He's not wedded to the idea. . .

"*Have you ever, sir, considered marriage?*"

There was a sudden flash of fire from Arriman's nostrils.

"*Marriage! Me marry! Are you out of your mind?*"

"*You could have a wizard baby, sir. Then it could take over from you. A son, you know,*" said Lester.

Arriman was silent. A son. For a moment he imagined the baby sitting in his pram, a dear little fellow tearing a marrow bone to shreds. Then he flinched.

"*Who would I marry?*" he muttered miserably.

But of course he knew. All of them knew. There is only one kind of person a wizard can marry, and that is a witch.

Which Witch?

Eva Ibbotson

illustrated by Annabel Large

SCHOLASTIC INC.

New York   Toronto   London   Auckland   Sydney
Mexico City   New Delhi   Hong Kong

ISBN 0-439-27061-8

12 11 10 9 8 7 6 5 4 3 2   0 1 2 3 4 5/0

Printed in the U.S.A.   40

First Scholastic printing, January 2001

For Alan

Which Witch?

CHAPTER 1

*A*S SOON AS he was born, Mr. and Mrs. Canker knew that their baby was not like other people's children.

For one thing, he was born with a full set of teeth and would lie in his pram for hours, chewing huge mutton bones to shreds or snapping at the noses of old ladies fool enough to kiss him. For another, though he screamed with temper when they changed his nappies, his eyes never actually filled with tears. Also—and perhaps this was the strangest of all—as soon as they brought him home from the hospital and lit a nice, bright fire in the sitting room, the smoke from their chimney began to blow *against* the wind.

For a while the Cankers were puzzled. But as Mr. Canker said, there is a book about *everything* if you only know where to look, and one day he went to Todcaster

Public Library and began to read. He read and he read and he read, and what he read most about was black magic and sorcery and how to tell from a very early age whether someone is going to be a wizard or a witch. After which, he went home and broke the news to Mrs. Canker.

It was a shock, of course. No one *likes* to think that their baby is going to grow up to be a wizard, and a black one at that. But the Cankers were sensible people. They changed the baby's name from George to Arriman (after a famous and very wicked Persian sorcerer), painted a frieze of vampire bats and newts' tongues on his nursery wall, and decided that if he had to grow up to be a wizard they would see to it he was a good one.

It wasn't easy. Todcaster, where they lived, was an ordinary town full of ordinary people. Though they encouraged little Arriman to practice as much as possible, it was embarrassing to have their birdbath full of gloomy and lopsided vultures and to have to explain to their neighbors why their apple tree had turned overnight into a blackened stump shaped like a dead man's hand.

Fortunately, wizards grow up quickly. By the time he was fifteen, Arriman could take a bus to Todcaster Common and raise a whirlwind that had every pair of knickers on every washing line in the area flying halfway to Jericho, and soon afterward he decided to leave home and set up on his own.

The search for a new house took many months. Arriman didn't want a place that was sunny and cheerful or a place that was near a town, and though he wanted somewhere ruined and desolate, he was fussy

about the kind of ghost it had. Never having had a sister, Arriman was a little shy with women, and he didn't fancy the idea of a wailing gray lady walking back and forth across his breakfast table while he ate his kippers, or a headless nun catching him in his bath.

But at last he found Darkington Hall. It was a gray, gloomy, sprawling building about thirty miles from Todcaster. To the west of the hall was a sinister forest, to the north were bleak and windswept moors, and to the east, the gray, relentlessly pounding sea. What's more, the Darkington ghost was a gentleman, and the sort that Arriman thought he could well get on with: Sir Simon Montpelier who, in the sixteenth century, had murdered all seven of his wives and now wandered about groaning with guilt, moaning with misery, and striking his forehead with a plashing sound.

And here Arriman lived for many years, blighting and smiting, blasting and wuthering, and doing everything he could to keep darkness and sorcery alive in the land. He filled his battlements with screech owls and his cellars with salamanders. He lined the avenue with scorched tree stumps like gallows, and he dug a well in his courtyard from which brimstone and sulfur oozed horribly. He planted a yew-tree maze so complicated and devilish that no one had a hope of coming out alive, and he made the fountains on the terrace run with blood. There was only one thing he couldn't do—he couldn't raise the ghost of Sir Simon Montpelier. He would have *liked* to do this; Sir Simon would have been company. But bringing ghosts back to life is the blackest and most difficult magic of all, and even Arriman couldn't manage it.

The years passed. Though he seldom left the hall, Arriman's fame was spreading. People called him Arriman the Awful. Loather of Light, and Wizard of the North. Stories began to be told about him: how he could make the thunder come before the lightning, that he was friends with Beelzebub himself. But Arriman just went on working. He had grown to be a tall and handsome man with dark, flashing eyes, a curved nose like the prow of a Viking ship, and a flourishing mustache, but despite his fine looks, he was not at all conceited.

In the years that followed, Arriman set up a private zoo in which he kept all the nastiest and ugliest animals he could find: monkeys with bald faces and blue behinds, camels with sneering lips and lumpy knees, wallabies with feet like railway sleepers that kicked everything in sight. He turned the billiard room into a laboratory in which fiendish things bubbled all day long, giving off appalling smells, and he called in rain clouds from the sea to drip relentlessly onto his roof.

Then one day he woke feeling completely miserable. He knew he ought to get up and throw someone into his well or order a stinking emu for the zoo or mix something poisonous in his laboratory, but he just couldn't face it.

"Lester," he said to the servant who brought him his breakfast. "I feel tired. Weary. Bored."

Lester was an ogre, a huge, slow-moving man with muscles like footballs. Like most ogres, he had only one eye in the middle of his forehead, but so as not to upset people he wore a black eye patch above it to make people think he had two. Before he came to be Arriman's servant, Lester had been a sword swallower in a fair, and he still liked to gulp down the odd saber or fencing foil. It soothed him.

Now he looked anxiously at his master. "Do you, sir?" he said.

"Yes, I do. In fact, I don't know if I can go on much longer. I thought I might go away somewhere, Lester. Take a little room in some pretty market town perhaps and write a book."

The ogre was shocked. "But what would happen to blackness and evil, sir?"

Arriman frowned. "I know, I know. I have a duty, I see that. But how long am I supposed to go on like this? How long, Lester?" The frown deepened and he waved his arms in desperation. "How *long*?"

Lester wasn't the stupid kind of ogre who goes around saying "Fe Fi Fo Fum" all the time. So now he looked at his master and said, "Well, I wouldn't know, sir. Ogres can't tell the future, you know. Gypsies can, though. Why don't you go and have your fortune told? There was a gypsy where I worked. Esmeralda, they called her. Knew her stuff, she did."

So the following week, Arriman and Lester drove into Todcaster to find the fair.

They found Esmeralda's caravan quite easily. You could tell it from the other gypsy caravans because the people who came out of it looked as though they didn't know what had hit them.

"She tells the truth," explained Lester, sniffing happily at the remembered fairground smells: fried onions from the hamburger stall, hot engine oil from the bumper cars. . . . "None of that garbage about dark strangers and journeys across the sea."

Esmeralda was a frizzy-haired lady in a pink satin blouse. Arriman had left off his magician's cloak and changed into a gray pinstripe, but the look she gave him was very sharp indeed.

"For you it'll be a fiver," she said. "Sit down."

She pocketed the money, took a swig from a bottle labeled Gordon's Gin, and began to stare into her crystal ball.

She stared for a long time. Then she pushed the ball away and lit a cigarette. "It's all right," she said. "He's coming."

"Who?" said Arriman eagerly. "Who's coming?"

"The new bloke," said Esmeralda. "The one that's going to take over from you."

Arriman looked bewildered. "What new bloke?"

Esmeralda closed her eyes wearily. "Do you want me to spell it out for you?" She put on a posh voice and droned: "Soon there cometh a great new wizard whose power shall be mightier and darker even than your own. When this great new wizard cometh, you, Arriman the Awful, will be able to lay down the burden of darkness and evil which you have carried for so long." She opened her eyes. "Got it?" she said nastily.

"Oh, yes, yes!" said Arriman happily. "I suppose you don't know *when* he cometh?"

"No," snapped Esmeralda, "I don't. Next customer, please."

After his visit to Esmeralda, Arriman was a happy man. Just to fill in time he planted a brier hedge whose thorns oozed blood, ran an oil tanker aground on the cliffs nearby, and invented a new spell for making people's hair fall out. But most of the time he spent by the main gate, watching and waiting for the new wizard to come.

It was cold work. Darkington Hall was as far north as you could get without bumping into Scotland, and when, after a week, Arriman found a chilblain on his left toe, he very sensibly decided to make a Wizard Watcher.

For the Wizard Watcher's body he used a sea lion shape, but larger and furrier with a sloping and rather cuddly chest. The Watcher had four feet and one tail, but it had three heads with keen-sighted and beautiful eyes set on short stalks. And every day at sunrise this gentle and very useful monster would waddle down the avenue, past the blackened trees shaped like gallows, past the oozing well and the devilish maze, and sit in the gateway watching for the wizard.

It watched in this way day after day, month after month, year after year, the Middle Head looking north over the moors, the Left Head looking west across the forest, and the Right Head looking east toward the sea. Then, on the nine hundred and nintieth day of just sitting there, the Wizard Watcher lost heart and became gloomy and annoyed.

"He cometh not from the north," said the Middle Head, as it had done every day for nine hundred and eighty-nine days.

"He cometh not from the west neither," said the Left Head.

"Nor from the east doesn't he cometh," said the Right Head. "And our feet are *freezing*."

"Our feet are blinking dropping *off*," said the Left Head.

There was a pause.

"Know what I think?" said the Middle Head. "I think the old man's been had."

"You mean there ain't going to *be* no new wizard?" said the Left Head.

The Middle Head nodded.

This time the pause was a long one.

"Don't fancy telling him," said the Right Head at last.

"Someone's got to," said the Middle Head.

So the monster turned and lumbered back to the hall, where it found Arriman in his bedroom dressing for dinner.

"Well?" he said eagerly. "What's the news?"

"The new wizard cometh not from the north," began the Middle Head patiently.

"Nor from the west he doesn't cometh," said the Left Head.

"And you can forget the east," said the Right Head, "because the new wizard doesn't cometh from there neither."

Then, speaking all together, the three heads said bravely: "We think you have been taken for a ride."

Arriman stared at them, aghast. "You can't mean it! It isn't possible!" He turned to Lester, who was getting ready to trim his master's mustache. "What do you think?"

The ogre rubbed his forehead under the eye patch and looked worried. "I've never known Esmeralda to make a mistake, sir. But it's been a long—"

He was interrupted by a terrible shriek from Arriman, who was peering forward into the mirror and clutching his head.

"A white hair!" yelled the magician. "A white hair in my curse curl! Oh, shades of darkness and perdition, this is the END!"

His shriek brought Mr. Leadbetter, his secretary, hurrying into the room. Mr. Leadbetter had been born with a small tail, which had made him think he was a demon. This was a silly thing to think because quite a lot of people have small tails. The Duke of Wellington had one and had to have a special hole made in his saddle when he rode to battle at Waterloo. But Mr. Leadbetter hadn't known about the Duke of Wellington and had wasted a lot of time trying to rob banks and so on, until he realized that crime didn't suit him and he became Arriman's secretary instead.

"Are you all right, sir?" he asked anxiously. "You seem upset."

"Upset? I'm finished! *Devastated.* Don't you know what a white hair means? It means old age, it means death. It means the end of wizardry and darkness and doom at Darkington. And where is the new wizard, where, where, *where*?"

The monster sighed. "He cometh not from the north," began the Middle Head wearily.

"I know he cometh not from the north, you dolt," snapped the Great Man. "That's exactly what I'm complaining about. What am I going to *do*? I can't wait forever."

Mr. Leadbetter coughed. "Have you ever, sir, considered marriage?"

There was a sudden flash of fire from Arriman's

nostrils, and from behind the paneling, Sir Simon gave a gurgling groan.

"Marriage! Me marry! Are you out of your *mind*?"

"If you were to marry, sir, it would ensure the succession," said Mr. Leadbetter calmly.

"What on earth are you talking about?" snapped Arriman, who was feeling thoroughly miserable and therefore cross.

"He means you could have a wizard baby, sir. Then it could take over from you. A son, you know," said Lester.

Arriman was silent. A son. For a moment he imagined the baby sitting in his pram, a dear little fellow tearing a marrow bone to shreds. Then he flinched.

"Who would I marry?" he muttered miserably.

But of course he knew. All of them knew. There is only one kind of person a wizard can marry, and that is a witch.

"It wouldn't be so bad, maybe?" said the Left Head encouragingly.

"Wouldn't be so *bad*!" yelled Arriman. "Are you out of your *mind*? A great black crone with warts and blisters in unmentionable places from crashing about on her broom! You want me to sit opposite one of *those* every morning eating my cornflakes?"

"I believe witches have changed since—" began Mr. Leadbetter.

But Arriman wouldn't listen. "Running along the corridors in her horrible nightgown, shrieking and flapping. Getting egg on her whiskers. Expecting her pussycat to sleep on the bed, no doubt!"

"She might not—"

"Every time I went to the kitchen for a snack she'd be there, stirring things in her filthy pot—rubbishy frogs' tongues and newts' eyes and all that balderdash. Never a decent bit of steak in the place, I expect, once she came."

"But—"

"Cleaning her foul yellow teeth in my washbasin," raged Arriman, getting more and more hysterical. "Or worse still, *not* cleaning her foul yellow teeth in my washbasin."

"She could have her own bathroom," said the Middle Head sensibly.

But nothing could stop Arriman, who stormed and ranted for another ten minutes. Then, turning suddenly very calm and pale, he said: "Very well, I see that it is my duty."

"A wise decision, sir," said his secretary.

"How shall I choose?" said Arriman. His voice was a mere thread. "It'll have to be a Todcaster witch, I suppose. Otherwise there's bound to be bad feeling. But how do we decide which witch?"

"As to that, sir," said Mr. Leadbetter, "I have an idea."

15

CHAPTER 2

THE WITCHES OF TODCASTER were preparing for a coven and they were very much excited. Covens are to witches what the Wolf Cubs or the Brownies are to people: a way of getting together and doing the things that interest them. And this one wasn't to be just an ordinary coven with feasting and dancing and wickedness. Rumors were going around that a most important announcement would be made.

"I wonder what it'll be," said Mabel Wrack. "Some new members, perhaps. We could do with them."

This was very true. Todcaster now had only seven proper witches. If Arriman had known what a state witchcraft had got to in the town of his birth he'd have been even more miserable than he was, but fortunately he didn't.

By day, Ms. Wrack kept a wet fish shop not far from

Todcaster Pier. She was a sea witch and never liked to be too far from the water. Ms. Wrack's mother, Mrs. Wrack, had been a mermaid: a proper one who lived on a rock and combed her hair and sang. But sailors had never been lured to their doom by her, partly because she looked like the back of a bus and partly because modern ships are so high out of the water that they never even saw her. So one day she had simply waddled out onto the beach at Todcaster Head with some sovereigns from a sunken galleon and persuaded a plastic surgeon who was on holiday there to operate on her tail and turn it into two legs.

It was from her mother that Mabel Wrack had her magic powers. From her father, Mr. Wrack, she had the shop.

Today she closed the shutters early, put a couple of cods' heads into a paper bag, and set off for her seaside bungalow. She was just turning into her road when she saw a group of children paddling happily in the surf.

"Tut!" said Ms. Wrack, pursing her lips. She closed her eyes, waved her paper bag with the cods' heads, and said some poetry. Almost at once a shoal of stinging jellyfish appeared in the water and the children ran screaming to their mothers.

"That's better," said Ms. Wrack. Like most witches, she hated happiness.

When she got home she went straight into her bedroom to change. Covens are like parties; what you wear is important. For this one, Ms. Wrack slipped into a purple robe embroidered all over in yellow cross-stitch haddocks, and fastened her best brooch—a single sea slug mounted in plastic—onto the band which kept her frizzy hair in place. Then she went into the bathroom.

"Come on, dear," she said, bending over the bath. "Time to get ready!"

What lived in Ms. Wrack's bath was, of course, her familiar. Familiars are the animals that help witches with their magic and are *exceedingly* important. Ms. Wrack's familiar was an octopus: a large animal with pale tentacles, suckers which left rings of blood where they had been, and vile red eyes. It was a girl octopus and its name was Doris.

"Now don't keep me waiting, dear," said Ms. Wrack. She had fetched a polyethylene bucket from the bathroom cupboard and was trying to stuff Doris inside. "Tonight's going to be an important night."

But Doris was in a playful mood. As soon as one tentacle was in, another was out, and it was a rather bedraggled Ms. Wrack who at last fixed on the lid, loaded the bucket onto an old perambulator, and set off for the coven bus.

Ethel Feedbag's familiar was not an octopus; it was a pig.

Ethel was a country witch who lived in a tumble-

down cottage in a village to the west of Todcaster. She was a round-faced, rather simple person who liked to hack at rutabagas with her spade, make parsnip wine, and shovel manure over absolutely everything, and just as people often grow to look like their dogs (or, the other way around), Ethel had grown to look very like her pig. Both of them had round, pink cheeks and very large behinds. Both of them moved slowly on short hairy legs and grunted as they went along, and both of them had dun-colored, sleepy little eyes.

Ethel had a job at the egg packing station. It was a boring job because the eggs she packed were mostly rotten anyway so there was nothing for her to do, but she filled in by giving the sheep husk and turning the cows dry as she bicycled home of an evening. As for the plants in the hedgerow between the egg packing station and Ethel's cottage, there was scarcely one that wasn't covered in mold or rust or hadn't clusters of greedy aphids sucking at its juices.

But tonight she rode straight home. Ethel was not a snappy dresser, but to make herself smart for the coven she rubbed down her Wellington boots with a handful of straw and changed her pinafore for a clean one with felt tomatoes (showing felt tomato blight) stitched to the pocket. Then she started looking for something she could take to eat. There didn't seem to be anything in the kitchen, but on the hearth rug in the living room she found a dead jackdaw which had fallen down the chimney.

"That'll roast a treat!" said Ethel, scooping it up. Then she went down to the shed at the bottom of her garden to fetch her pig.

Nancy and Nora Shouter were twin witches who worked at Todcaster Central Station. They were an unusually disagreeable pair who hated passengers, hated each other, and hated trains. As soon as Nancy went to the loudspeaker and announced that the seven fifty-two to Edinburgh was approaching platform nine, Nora rushed to *her* loudspeaker and cackled into it that the seven fifty-two had engine trouble and would be ninety minutes late and then it wouldn't approach platform nine at all but would come in at platform five, *if* they were lucky.

So now, when they should have been getting ready for the coven, they were standing in their underclothes in the bedroom of their flat in Station Road, arguing about which of their familiars was which.

"That is *so* my chicken!" shouted Nora, tugging at the tail feathers of the unfortunate bird.

"That is *not* your chicken," shrieked Nora. "*That* is your chicken over there!"

It was a most ridiculous argument. The Shouter girls were identical, with dyed red hair, long noses, and smoke-stained fingertips. They dressed alike and slept in twin beds and they both had chickens for familiars, which lived in wicker crates beneath their beds. And, of course, the chickens, too, were very much alike. Chickens often are—fidgety brown birds who would peck your fingers as soon as look at you. But none of this made any difference to the Shouter twins, who went on bickering so long that they were very nearly late for the most important coven of their lives.

For many years now, the witches of Todcaster had met on Windylow Heath, a wild, wuthering sort of place with a few stunted thorn trees, a pond in which a gloomy lady had drowned herself on her wedding eve, and a single rock on which the ancient druids had done some dreadful deeds.

To get there, the witches hired a bus—the Coven Special—which left the bus depot at seven P.M. (No one had flown on a broomstick since a witch called Mrs. Hockeridge had been sucked down the ventilation shaft of a Boeing 707 from Heathrow to Istanbul and nearly caused a very nasty mess indeed.)

The Shouter twins were still quarreling when they got to the depot, but they stopped when they saw, standing on the pavement beside the bus, a small brown coffee table.

"It's her again," said Nancy.

"Silly old crone," said Nora.

"I've a good mind to stub out my cigarette on her," said Nancy, who as usual had one dangling from her lips.

They glared at the squat, round table, which seemed to be swaying a little from side to side.

" 'Tis a pity when they go simple like that," said Ethel Feedbag. She had loaded her pig onto the trailer and now came over and prodded the table leg with her Wellington boot.

The coffee table was in fact a very old witch called Mother Bloodwort, who lived in a tumbledown shack near a disused quarry in the poorest part of town.

When she was young, Mother Bloodwort had been a

formidable witch of the old school, bringing people out in boils, putting the evil eye on butchers who sold her gristly chops, and casting spells on babies in perambulators so that their own mothers didn't know them.

But now she was old. Her memory had gone, and like many old people she got fancies. One of her fancies was to turn herself into a coffee table. There was no point in her being a coffee table: Mother Bloodwort did not drink coffee, which was far too expensive, and since she lived alone there was no one who might have wanted to put a cup and saucer down on her. But she was a cranky old witch and every so often she remembered the spell that changed her from a white-haired, whiskery old woman into a low, oak table with carved legs and a glass top, and then there was no stopping her. What she did *not* often remember was how to turn herself back again.

"Oh, come along," called Mabel Wrack from inside the bus. "Leave the silly old thing where she is."

From her mermaid mother Mabel had inherited rather scaly legs that dried out easily and itched, so she wanted to get to Windylow Heath where the air was damp and cool.

But just then something happened. Two sparrows who'd been squabbling in the gutter lifted their heads and began to sing like nightingales. A flock of golden butterflies appeared from nowhere, and drifting through the grimy bus station came the scent of primroses with morning dew on them.

"Ugh! It's her!" said Nancy Shouter. "I'm off." And she threw her chicken into the trailer and climbed into the bus.

"Me too," said her twin. "I can't *stand* her. I don't know why they allow her in the coven. Really I don't."

Belladonna came slowly around the corner. She was a very young witch with thick, golden hair in which a short-eared bat hung like a little wrinkled prune. There was usually *something* in Belladonna's hair: a fledgling blackbird parked there by its mother while she went to hunt for worms, a baby squirrel wanting somewhere safe to eat its hazelnuts, or a butterfly who thought she was a lily or a rose. Belladonna's nose turned up at the end, making a ledge for tired ladybirds to rest on; she had a high, clear forehead and eyes as blue as periwinkles. But as she came up to the bus she hesitated and looked troubled and sad, for she had learned to expect only unkindness from the other witches.

Then she saw the coffee table and forgot her own troubles at once.

"Oh, *poor* Mother Bloodwort! Have you forgotten the undoing spell again?"

The table began to rock and Belladonna put her arms around it. "Try to think," she said. "I'm sure you can remember. Was it a rhyming spell?"

The table rocked harder.

"It was? Well, I'm *sure* it'll come back in a minute." She leaned her cheek against the glass top, sending healing thoughts into the old witch's tired brain. "It's coming back, I can *feel* it coming back. . . ."

There was a swishing noise, Belladonna tumbled backward, and there, standing before her, was an old woman in a long mouse-bitten cloak and felt bedroom slippers with the sides cut out.

"Thank you, my dear," croaked Mother Bloodwort. "You're a kind girl even if you are—"

But she couldn't bring herself to say the dreadful word—no black witch can. So she hobbled to the bus and began to heave herself aboard, clutching to her chest a large, square tin showing a picture of King George VI's coronation on the lid. The tin *should* have gone in the trailer—there was a rule that all familiars traveled separately—but Mother Bloodwort never let it out of her sight. Inside it were hundreds of large white maggots which, when you blew on them, turned into a cloud of flies. *One* fly is no good for magic, but a cloud of flies—flies in your hair, your eyes, your nose—that makes a very good familiar indeed.

Belladonna was the last to get into the bus. She alone of all the witches had no familiar. For white magic you do not need one. It was another thing that made her feel so very much alone.

25

CHAPTER 3

BELLADONNA HAD ALWAYS been a white witch. Even as a tiny baby she had used her teeth only to bite the tops off milk bottles so that the bluetits could get at the cream, and as she grew older her whiteness grew steadily worse. Flowers sprang up where she walked, bursts of glorious music fell from the air, and when she smiled, old gentlemen remembered the Christmases they had had when they were children. As for her hair—from the age of six or so when it had reached her waist, there had always been *someone* resting in Belladonna's golden hair.

Belladonna herself longed for blackness—to smite and blast and wreck and wither seemed to her the most wonderful thing in the world. But though she could heal people and charm the flowers out of the ground and speak the language of the animals, even the simplest bit of evil, like, say, turning a pale green cucumber into a greasy black pudding with bits of fat in it, was more than she could manage. Not that she didn't try. Every morning before she went to work (she was an assistant in a flower shop), Belladonna would stand by the open window and say: "Every day and in every way I am getting blacker and blacker."

But she wasn't, and the worst thing she had to bear was the scorn and spite of the other witches. Belladonna really dreaded coven days when she was ignored and despised and had to huddle by herself out of the warm circle of firelight and feasting with only the familiars for company. The only reason she went was that she hoped, one day, some of the blackness might rub off on her.

The bus had left Todcaster now. There was one more witch to pick up on the way. She was a thin, pale witch whom the others called Monalot after a lady on a radio program who was always complaining. Monalot's real name was Gwendolyn Swamp and she played the harp in the Todcaster Palm Orchestra. Ms. Swamp came from a family of banshees, who are the kind of witch who wails and sighs about the place and tells people when something awful is going to happen. Banshees have never been a healthy bunch, and Monalot was so often ill that to get her to the coven at all they usually stopped the bus specially by her house.

"She's not at the gate," said Mabel Wrack impatiently. The air-conditioning in the Coven Special was making her legs itch unbearably.

So Belladonna, who always took the messages and ran the errands for the others, climbed out of the bus and walked through the garden of Monalot's little villa with the name Creepy Corner written on the gate.

The door was open. Belladonna ran up to the bedroom, knocked on the door—and saw at once that Monalot would not be coming to the coven. The poor witch was completely covered in small red spots.

"It's the measles," she moaned. "All over me. Percy, too." She waved a limp hand to the corner of the room where her familiar, a large, sad-looking sheep, was lying. A sheep with measles is unusual, but where there is witchcraft anything is possible.

Belladonna was very upset.

"Couldn't I help?" she began.

But like most witches, Monalot hated the word "help." "No," she moaned. "Just go and leave me. No one wants me anyway, nobody cares."

So Belladonna poured her a drink, plumped up her pillows, and went out, passing, on Monalot's dressing table, wax images of her doctor and the district nurse, both stuck full of pins.

"I'm afraid it's hopeless," she reported, back in the bus. "Ms. Swamp has the measles."

"Stupid old banshee," snapped Nora Shouter.

"They were always delicate, the Swamps," said Mother Bloodwort. She had opened her tin with the coronation on the lid and was stirring her maggots with a long and bony finger. She was still stirring and muttering when the bus got to Windylow Heath.

Two hours later the coven was in full swing. In the middle of the heath, the bonfire roared and crackled, lighting up the Great Rock on which the ancient druids had done their dreadful deeds. The smell of burnt feathers from Ethel Feedbag's roasted jackdaw rose hideously on the night air; clouds passed to and fro across the fitful moon. The witches had finished feasting and singing rude songs (the kind where "owl" doesn't just rhyme with "howl," but with things like "bowel" or "foul") and were dancing back to back, or trying to. Ethel Feedbag's Wellingtons did not help, nor the size of her behind as she lurched round with Mabel Wrack.

"You're going the wrong way, you stupid stick," yelled Nancy over her shoulder to her twin. "It's widdershins we should be going."

"This *is* widdershins, you half-witted cowpat," Nora screamed back.

Mother Bloodwort did not dance anymore. She sat as close to the fire as she could get, her mouse-bitten robe turned back so that the heat could get at her gnarled old legs. Every so often a handful of the flies that buzzed drunkenly round her head fell into the flames and vanished.

As for Belladonna, as usual she was left out in the cold. No one wanted to dance with her, and anyway, like mothers who hand their children over to nannies and nursemaids, the witches had told Belladonna to take their familiars away to a little clump of thorn trees and keep them quiet.

This was easier said than done. As soon as the familiars saw Belladonna they always went to pieces. Ethel Feedbag's enormous pig had collapsed like a felled tree and was lying on its back, its legs in the air, squealing for her to scratch its stomach. The Shouter chickens, who hadn't laid anything in years, began to puff out their feathers and squawk, trying to please her with an egg. And Doris the octopus stuck a tentacle out of her plastic bucket and laid it softly on Belladonna's knee.

Meanwhile, over by the fire, the witches grew wilder and wilder. Mother Bloodwort was knocking back a bottle of black liquid labeled Furniture Polish: Not for Human Consumption. Mabel Wrack was kicking her scaly legs higher and higher, showing off her garters of lungfish skin. The Shouter twins were hacking at each other's shins.

And then, suddenly, something happened.

First there came—from the very depths of the earth it seemed—a low and sinister rumbling. Then the ground began to shake and shiver and a dreadful crack appeared beneath the Great Rock of the druids.

"It's an earthquake," yelled Mabel Wrack, and the witches threw themselves on the ground, gibbering with fear.

Next came a thunderclap, louder than any they had ever heard, followed by a streak of forked lightning so brilliant that it turned night to day.

"The thunder before the lightning!" wailed Mother Bloodwort, and began to beat her white old head against the ground.

After that came the fog, a great, yellow, choking, blinding fog which rolled across the heath, enveloping everything in its cold and smothering darkness.

"It be t'end of the world," wailed Ethel Feedbag.

"It's the Creeping Death," shrieked Nora Shouter.

Only Belladonna was still on her feet, trying to comfort the terrified familiars.

Then, as suddenly as it had come, the great fog rolled away, there was a last clap of thunder—and the witches gasped.

31

For there, standing astride the Great Rock of the druids, was a figure so splendid, so magnificent, that it quite took their breath away.

Arriman had taken a lot of trouble with his clothes. He wore a flowing mantle embroidered with the constellations of the planets, his trousers were of gold lamé, and he wore not just horns but antlers, which Lester had fastened most cunningly behind his ears. With his devilish eyebrows, his soaring mustache, and the sulfurous glow that surrounded him, he presented a vision from which one simply could not tear one's eyes.

"Greetings, ye foulmouthed hags and lovers of darkness!" boomed the great magician.

"Greetings!" croaked the witches, rising slowly to their feet.

Arriman could not see Belladonna, who was hidden behind a thorn tree, but he could see Mabel Wrack, whose sea slug had fallen over one eye, and Ethel Feedbag, a burnt jackdaw feather sticking to her chin. He could see Mother Bloodwort and he could see the Shouter twins, and when he'd seen them he turned and tried to scramble down the rock.

"Steady, sir," said Mr. Leadbetter, who was standing behind the rock with a sheaf of papers.

"The Cankers have never been quitters, sir," said Lester, placing a huge hand on his master's shoulder.

Seeing his retreat cut off, Arriman reluctantly climbed up the rock again. The witches meanwhile were getting dreadfully excited. They had begun to realize that they were in the presence of the Great Wizard of the North, whom nobody had seen for years and years and years and whose power was the greatest in the land.

"Know ye," Arriman went on bravely, "that I am Arriman the Awful, Loather of Light and Blighter of the Beautiful."

"Know we. I mean, we know," croaked the witches.

"Know ye also that, obedient to the prophecy of the gypsy Esmeralda, I have waited nine hundred and ninety days for the coming of the new wizard to Darkington Hall." He caught a whiff of manure from Ethel Feedbag's Wellingtons and staggered backward.

"Bear up, sir," came Lester's voice from the darkness behind him, and with a great effort, Arriman pulled himself together and went on.

"Know ye also that the aforesaid wizard not having turned up, I, Arriman Frederick Canker, have decided to take a wife."

The excitement of the witches grew to a frenzy. They began to mutter and nudge each other and to cackle fiendishly because it was known that Arriman had sworn never to marry. Only Belladonna went on standing quietly in the shelter of the trees, her periwinkle eyes fixed wonderingly on the great magician.

"Know ye," Arriman went on, bracing himself, "that for my bride I have decided to choose a witch of Todcaster and that whichever witch I choose shall reign—" His voice broke. "I can't do it," he murmured, passing a hand across his eyes. He had just caught sight of Mother Bloodwort's fly-covered whiskers in a sudden spurt of firelight.

"No use turning back now, sir," came Mr. Leadbetter's quiet voice. But both the secretary and the ogre, peering out behind the rock, were very much upset. They had had no idea that things had got so bad in Todcaster.

So Arriman made a last desperate effort. "Know ye," he went on, "that to choose which witch shall be my bride, I have arranged a great competition on the grounds of my estate at Darkington during the fearful week of Halloween. And know ye that whichever witch does there the vilest, darkest, and most powerful piece of magic shall be my wife!"

Pandemonium now broke out. Arriman waited for the lurching, cackling, and hiccuping to die down and then he said: "Mr. Leadbetter, my secretary, will stay behind to give you your instructions for the contest. And remember," he said, throwing out his arms, "that what I am looking for is power, wickedness, and evil. Darkness is All!"

And with a sigh of relief, Arriman vanished.

When the witches had calmed down again, Mr. Leadbetter stepped out from behind the rock and handed everyone an entry form for the contest. Mother Bloodwort, who couldn't read, held hers upside down, and the Shouter twins immediately began arguing about how many days there were to Halloween.

"What about that lady over there?" said Mr. Leadbetter. He had caught sight of the pale glimmer of Belladonna's hair between the trees.

"Oh, you don't want to bother with *her*," said Nancy Shouter.

"She's not one of us," said her twin.

"Still, she is a witch," said Mother Bloodwort, spitting out a couple of flies. She was the only one who sometimes had a kind word for Belladonna. So Mr. Leadbetter walked over to the clump of trees where Belladonna was still trying to calm the familiars.

"Oh, dear," he said when he had introduced himself. "How *very* unfortunate."

For he realized as soon as he saw her what was wrong. The little, short-eared bat hanging so tenderly in her hair, the chickens roosting on her feet, the scent of primroses with morning dew on them. "Have you . . . er . . . always been . . .?"

"White?" said Belladonna sadly. "Yes. From birth."

"Nothing can be done, I suppose?"

Belladonna shook her head. "I've tried everything."

"You won't be going in for the contest, then?"

Belladonna shook her head. "What would be the use? You heard him. 'Darkness is All,' he said." Witches cannot cry any more than wizards can, but her eyes were wide with sorrow. "Tell me, is he really . . . as marvelous as he looks?"

Mr. Leadbetter thought. Pictures came into his mind. Arriman shrieking with rage when he lost his suspenders. Arriman filling the bath with electric eels and giggling. Arriman ordering twelve stinking emus for the zoo and leaving his secretary to unpack them . . . But there was nothing mean or small-spirited about Arriman, and it was very sincerely that Mr. Leadbetter said: "He is a gentleman. Most truly a gentleman."

"I thought he must be," said Belladonna, sighing.

"Well, I'll leave you one of these anyway, in case you change your mind," he said. "And perhaps you'd be kind enough to see that—Ms. Swamp, is it—gets hers, too?" He had turned away when he remembered something. "I'm going to vanish in a minute," he said. "At least I hope I am. I don't have any magic powers myself so I hope the great man will remember. But when I do there'll be some presents on the rock—one for each witch. Make sure you get yours."

"Oh, thank you, I will," said Belladonna. Then she added shyly: "I hope you don't mind my saying so, but when you walked away just now I thought how *very* good-looking it was. Your tail, I mean. Mostly the backs of gentlemen are so flat and dull."

Mr. Leadbetter was very much moved. "Thank you, my dear; you've made me very happy. Of course the moonlight is flattering. By daylight it can look a little crude."

He pressed her hand gratefully. It was on the tip of his tongue to tell her about his childhood and the shock of finding that he was not like other boys, but just then Arriman found he needed his secretary. There was a little puff of smoke and Mr. Leadbetter vanished.

Almost at once, the other witches began to shriek and yammer.

"Look! Over there, on the rock!"

"Something glittering!"

The next second they were all scrambling at a pile of oval hand mirrors, very beautiful ones, set in frames of precious stones. But when they looked into the mirrors' shining surfaces they did not see their own ugly faces. They saw the face of the great Arriman with his flashing eyes and curving nose and magnificent mustache. What was more, the mirror showed the witches what Arriman was doing at any moment in time so that they could get to know him and his habits and know what awaited them at Darkington if they should win.

"What a smasher!" said Nora Shouter.

"Well, you're not going to win, *I'm* going to win!"

"Cor, I wouldn't mind being married to 'im," said Ethel Feedbag. "Give the sheep the staggers, I will, when I get up there—an' the cows the bloat."

Mabel Wrack smiled pityingly. The daughter of Mrs. Wrack, who'd been a mermaid, was such an obvious winner that she had nothing at all to worry about. "Mabel Canker, Wizardess of the North." It sounded good.

"I never thought I'd be glad I buried poor Mr. Bloodwort," said Mother Bloodwort. "But I am because now I can go in for the competition."

"You!" shrieked the Shouter twins. "You're far too old!"

"I am now," said Mother Bloodwort, "though there's a lot of men as likes an older woman. But I've got a turning-myself-young-again spell. It's on the tip of my tongue, and when I remember it I won't half make things hum!"

Belladonna had crept shyly forward and picked up one of the two mirrors that still glittered on the rock. Arriman was taking off his antlers—she could just see Lester's huge hand undoing the tape. The great man looked tired and discouraged. Oh, if only she could be there to stroke his forehead and comfort him!

"What are *you* hanging round for?" said Mabel

Wrack. "*You* won't be going in for the competition."

"That'd be a joke. Blossoming roses in the snow! Golden singing birds! *Yak!*" said Nora Shouter.

Belladonna said nothing. In silence, she helped the other witches pack up their picnics, lifted Doris into the trailer, soothed Ethel Feedbag's pig. But when the bus was ready to leave, she did not join the others. It was a long walk back to Todcaster in the darkness, but she welcomed the idea of it. More than anything, she wanted to be alone.

She was sitting quietly on the rock where he had stood, gazing into the mirror, when a high and irritable voice said: "Well, I think you're just being wet. Wet and feeble."

Belladonna sat up, startled. Then she realized that the voice had spoken not "human" but "bat" and had come from her own hair.

"Not to say spineless," the little bat went on. "Why don't you at least have a *try*?"

"Don't be silly," said Belladonna. "You know perfectly well that I can't even make a toad come out of someone's mouth, and that's the corniest piece of blackness there is."

"People change," said the bat. "Take my Aunt Screwtooth. She was the most useless old bat you can imagine—couldn't suck juice out of an overripe pear without her husband to hold her claw. Then they took a holiday in some place abroad. Transylvania or some such name. She fell in with a family of vampires and settled over there. You should see her now, sucking blood as if it were mother's milk. Fairly sozzled with the stuff she is. And if my Aunt Screwtooth, why not you?"

Belladonna was bending over the mirror again. Arriman was in his pajamas now. Yellow silk, they were, edged with black braid.

"Is that really true? About your Aunt Screwtooth?"

The little bat blushed in the darkness. He had made the whole thing up because he loved Belladonna.

But Belladonna did not see. She was thinking. If she went in for the contest she could at least *see* him again. He'd be one of the judges for sure. And once she was there, maybe she'd find *some* way to help and comfort him.

She stood up. "All right," she said, "I'll do it. I'll have a try."

CHAPTER 4

*M*R. LEADBETTER WAS very fond of watching television. In spite of his little stump of a tail he was a very ordinary person, and when the magic and goings-on at Darkington were too much for him, he liked to go quietly to his room and watch the box.

One of Mr. Leadbetter's favorite programs was the Miss World competition. Mr. Leadbetter knew, of course, that it was silly for girls to let themselves be prodded and measured like cows or turnips at an agricultural show, but all the same he very much liked all the contestants coming from different countries and staying together at a hotel and appearing first in their national costumes and then in their evening dresses and then in their swimsuits, and when the most beautiful one climbed onto the platform and had a crown put on her head, Mr. Leadbetter always felt a lump come to his throat.

So when it was decided to hold a competition for the blackest witch of Todcaster, Mr. Leadbetter decided to organize it rather in the way that the Miss World contest was organized. Not, of course, that he thought of making the witches parade in their swimsuits. Even before he saw Mother Bloodwort and Mabel Wrack and Ethel Feedbag he had not thought of *that*. But it seemed to him a good idea that the witches should be brought together in a hotel first and get their clothes and their table manners sorted out before they got to Darkington. Above all, he wanted to make sure that they knew the rules and that no hanky-panky went on between them. Any witch casting a spell on another witch was to be disqualified *immediately*.

So he rented the Grand Spa Hotel on the outskirts of Todcaster. It was a very grand hotel with a cocktail lounge and a ballroom and a terrace with stripy deck chairs, and the manager, who was quite used to conferences of politicians and schoolteachers and clergymen, rather welcomed the idea of a conference of witches.

But after his first day there, Mr. Leadbetter began to feel that he had made a terrible mistake. Mother Bloodwort and the Shouter twins and Ethel Feedbag just did not *behave* like Miss Kenya and Miss Belgium and Miss U.S.A. In fact, as Mr. Leadbetter said to Lester, who had come to help him, if it wasn't for Belladonna he'd have had a good mind to chuck the whole thing and let Arriman get on with choosing his own wife.

Belladonna, who had arrived earlier carrying a straw basket with her toothbrush, her nightdress, and the magic mirror, had been wonderful. It was Belladonna who had tactfully removed Ethel Feedbag's Wellies and hosed them down in the pantry when the manager complained about manure on his carpet. It was Belladonna who had taped up Mother Bloodwort's tin with the coronation on the lid and persuaded the old woman that at the best hotels one did not come down to dinner in a cloud of flies. And when Mabel Wrack got into the bath fully clothed because her legs were drying out, causing Doris (who liked to be alone) to squirt her all over with inky fluid, it was Belladonna who cleaned up the mess and carried the irritated animal to her own bathroom and quieted her.

Not that she got any thanks for it. "It makes my blood boil," said Lester, "the way those witches talk to you."

"Oh, well," said Belladonna. "It's hard for them, me being . . . you know . . ."

They were in the office, which the manager had kindly lent to Mr. Leadbetter, snatching a quick cup of tea. Lester, who'd been badly hit by the sight of the witches in daylight, was prowling around looking for a sword to swallow. Mr. Leadbetter, like everyone who organizes things, was shuffling his papers and worrying.

"Maybe you're just *fancying* yourself white," Lester went on. He found the manager's umbrella, looked at it, and put it down again. There wasn't any real skill in swallowing umbrellas, and if they came unfurled inside it could be messy.

"I'm afraid not," said Belladonna. As usual she was looking into the magic mirror, which she carried with her everywhere. Arriman was sitting hunched up in what seemed to be a broom cupboard.

"Try!" said Lester, who'd set his heart on Belladonna as mistress of Darkington Hall. "Look, see that typewriter on the desk? Bet if you really put your mind to it you could turn it into a nest of vipers or something. I mean, you've got to *believe* in yourself."

Belladonna sighed. She knew it was useless but she hated disappointing people, so she got up and felt in the pocket of her skirt for a magic wand or something of the sort. There wasn't anything, of course—only a handful of healing herbs, the identity disk of a carrier pigeon who was playing truant from his loft, and a baby field mouse. So she put everything back and just closed her eyes, waved her arms over the typewriter, and thought of the blackest things she could think of, such as uncooked liver and shoelaces and open graves. Then she stepped back.

"Oh, dear!" said Mr. Leadbetter.

The typewriter had not turned into a nest of vipers. It had turned into a pot of pink begonias; charming, sweetly scented flowers, each cradling a golden bee.

"Pretty," said the ogre gloomily.

"I told you," said Belladonna, very much embarrassed. She turned the typewriter back again and picked up the magic mirror. How dreadfully the great man would despise her if he knew!

"Still sulking, is he?" said Lester.

"Oh, no, he could never *sulk*," said Belladonna. "But he hasn't perhaps been very . . . *cheerful* lately."

"You can say that again," said the ogre.

And indeed, ever since he had seen his choice of future brides at the coven, Arriman had been in a terrible state. He woke screaming from dreadful nightmares, babbling of fly-covered whiskers chasing him down corridors. He was off his food, his mustache had begun to molt, and he hounded the Wizard Watcher unmercifully, sending the poor beast out to the gate long before daybreak in a last, desperate hope that the new wizard might still come and he could cancel the competition.

"I can't help wondering why he is sitting in a *broom* cupboard," said Belladonna.

"I'll tell you why," said Lester frowning. "Because he's waiting for Sir Simon, that's why. Favorite spot of Sir Simon's, the broom cupboard."

"Is that the rather dead-looking gentleman he speaks to sometimes?" inquired Belladonna.

Lester nodded. "Very dead-looking. Died in 1583," he said. "Murdered all seven of his wives."

Mr. Leadbetter put down his papers and came over, and together the ogre and the secretary looked over Belladonna's shoulder at their employer. Sure enough, a wavering shadow appeared on the surface of the mirror and Arriman rose eagerly to his feet.

"I don't like it," said Lester, shaking his enormous head. "He's been trying to bring Sir Simon back to life for years, but since the coven he's been at it all the time. When I brought him his egg this morning, he was sitting up in bed with this huge book—*Necromancy*, it was called. Nasty."

"I wouldn't worry," said Mr. Leadbetter. "I believe it's two hundred years since anyone managed to raise a ghost."

But he was a little more anxious than he admitted. Suppose Arriman *did* manage it? A man who had murdered all seven of his wives did not seem to be a good person to have around in a house where there was soon to be a wedding.

An hour later the witches were all assembled in the cocktail lounge of the hotel waiting for Mr. Leadbetter to tell them the rules of the contest. They had taken a lot of trouble to make themselves smart. Mabel Wrack had plaited her frizzy hair with a string of dogfish egg cases, Mother Bloodwort's chin sprouted a brand-new bandage, and Ethel Feedbag had nobly left her Wellies upstairs and was in slippers.

"Are we all here?" asked Mr. Leadbetter, letting his eyes rest for a moment on Belladonna, sitting quietly apart from the others on a stool.

"No," said Nancy Shouter, jangling her knuckle-bone earrings. "Silly old Monalot's not here."

Mr. Leadbetter sighed. Ms. Swamp had sent in her entrance form, but so far there had been no sign of her, and he was a person who hated muddle.

"No point in her going in for the competition anyway," said Mabel Wrack. "A flabby old banshee like that."

"And that sheep of hers. Gives me the bots!" said Ethel Feedbag.

The others nodded. It was true that Percy really was a most depressing animal: the kind that always thinks other sheep are having a better life than he is, and eating greener grass, and *doing* more.

"Well, we shall have to begin without her," said Mr. Leadbetter.

But just then the hotel porter came in and whispered something to Mr. Leadbetter, whose face brightened. "Show her in, please," he said. "We're expecting another lady."

But the new witch didn't seem to be someone one showed in. The new witch came striding in like a queen, and as she came the other witches shrank back in their chairs and Belladonna drew in her breath.

Because the new witch was not Monalot. Nothing less like the pale, sickly Ms. Swamp could be imagined. The new witch was very tall, with black hair piled high on her head. She had long, bloodred fingernails, and round her shoulders she wore a cape of puppy skin. Her fingers and wrists sparkled with jewels, but the necklace wound round her throat was, unexpectedly, not of pearls or diamonds but of human teeth. But what startled the others most was the new witch's familiar. Dragging behind her on a rhinestone-studded lead there came a gray, lumbering animal with a snout like a Hoover and wicked-looking claws.

"What is it?" whispered Mother Bloodwort, who could never scrape up enough money to go to the zoo.

"I think it's an aardvark," Belladonna whispered back.

"Good evening," said the new witch. "I am Madame Olympia. I have come to take part in the competition."

"I'm afraid there's been some mistake," said Mr. Leadbetter. "The competition is limited to the witches of Todcaster."

Madame Olympia smiled—a smile that sent shivers down one's spine.

"I *am* a witch of Todcaster," she said.

"How can that be?" began Mr. Leadbetter. "We—"

"I have bought Ms. Gwendolyn Swamp's house, Creepy Corner," interrupted the newcomer, dropping the rhinestone lead carelessly onto a chair. "Too small for me, of course, but not without charm. Miss Swamp found she wanted to travel."

"Monalot *never* wanted to travel," said Mother Bloodwort stoutly. "Travel brought her out in spots an' all sorts. It was all you could do to get Monalot down the road for a bag of bulls' eyes."

"She is traveling now, however," said Madame Olympia with another of her sinister smiles. "Oh, yes, she is definitely traveling now. Somewhere around Turkey, I would guess."

She opened her crocodile-skin handbag and began to powder her nose. And when she saw the vain, proud look that Madame Olympia threw at herself in the mirror, Belladonna suddenly understood what kind of a person the new witch was. She was an enchantress, one of the oldest and most evil kinds of witch there is. Morgan le Fay, the one who caused the death of the great King Arthur, was one, and Circe, who turned brave Ulysses' men to swine. Enchantresses are beautiful, but it is an evil beauty. They use it to snare men and make them helpless and tear from them the secrets of their power. And when they have got all they want from them, they destroy them.

"Well, madame, I suppose you had better let me have your entrance form," said Mr. Leadbetter. Fair was fair, and if the new witch now lived in Todcaster she was eligible to join. But he felt very unhappy as he wrote her name down on the register. Mr. Leadbetter didn't know much about enchantresses, but there was something about Madame Olympia that made his blood run cold.

Not only was Madame Olympia not a witch of Todcaster, she wasn't a Witch of the North at all. She lived in London, where she kept a beauty parlor. It was a wicked place. Stupid women were lured into it and assured they would become young and beautiful if they let themselves be pummeled and pounded and smeared with sticky creams, and have their faces lifted and their stomachs flattened. They paid a lot of money to Madame Olympia, who would put a little bit of magic into the creams and ointments that she used so that at first they did look marvelous. But it was the kind of magic that wore off very quickly, leaving the women even uglier than before so that they would rush back to her and pay her more money and the whole thing would start again. She was also horrid to the girls she employed and paid them too little and bullied them.

Madame Olympia had had five husbands. All these husbands had disappeared in very odd ways, mostly after they had made wills leaving her all their money. She *said* that they had died, but it was odd that a werewolf with weak, blue eyes and a bald patch had appeared in Epping Forest, very much frightening the inhabitants, just after she had reported her first husband's death. The second and third husbands had vanished within a year of each other, and each time the girls in the beauty parlor were struck by the way madame's necklace of human teeth suddenly got very much longer. The fourth Mr. Olympia really did run his Jaguar into a lamppost, but the fifth . . . well, no one knew for certain what had happened to him, but the coffin in which he was carried to his funeral was most *suspiciously* light.

And now she was after Arriman the Awful, Wizard of the North!

As soon as she had heard of the competition she had come straight up to Todcaster and "persuaded" Monalot to sell her house. Monalot hadn't wanted to go, of course: she'd sobbed and moaned and pleaded; after all, she wasn't a banshee for nothing. But by the time Madame Olympia had suggested just a few of the things she might do to her, and to Percy, if she didn't, Monalot had been very glad to sell her house and take a nice package tour round the world. Very glad indeed.

Mr. Leadbetter had begun to explain the rules of the competition. The witches were to wear black gowns and masks so that the judges would not go by the way they looked but by the blackness of their magic. They were to draw numbers out of a hat and do their tricks in the order that they drew. They were to hand in a list of anything they might need for the contest: dragons' blood, sieves to go to sea in, and so on, so that they would be ready in good time. . . .

Madame Olympia hardly bothered to listen. One look at the other witches and she had known she would win. The little golden-haired thing was quite fetching, but anyone could see what was wrong with *her*. Oh, yes, she'd be Queen of Darkington all right. And then . . . !

Hardly waiting for Mr. Leadbetter to finish, she rose to her feet and stretched. "See that my aardvark is watered and fed, please," she ordered carelessly. "I'm going to change for dinner."

And she glided out of the room, leaving the other witches boiling and bubbling with indignation.

"Cocky, sneering cow, who does she think she is?" said Nancy Shouter. "Hope she drops dead."

And for once, her twin agreed with her.

It was a long time before Belladonna slept that night. Dinner had been excellent, but even before the bandage fell from Mother Bloodwort's chin into her mushroom soup, Belladonna had not been really hungry. Then there was a fuss about Ethel Feedbag, who had a double bed and wanted to share it with her pig, and when Belladonna got to her room at last there was still Doris in the bath, waving to her and wanting to be noticed.

But it was none of that that worried Belladonna. It was the glimpse she had had, passing an open door, of Madame Olympia, standing in a gold negligee, her black hair falling round her shoulders, the aardvark cowering at her feet. She was looking into the magic mirror that had been left for Monalot and laughing—a low and truly evil sound.

"You wanted power and darkness, you Wizard of the North," Belladonna heard her say. "Well, power and darkness you shall have!"

And it was with the sound of the new witch's horrible laughter still in her ears that Belladonna fell asleep at last.

CHAPTER 5

B ELLADONNA WAS still worried when she awoke. It seemed to her certain that Madame Olympia would win the competition and become Mrs. Canker, and she feared most dreadfully for Arriman.

She got up and went to the open window, and at once a family of bluetits flew onto her shoulder and started telling her a long story about a nesting box that wasn't fit for a flea to sleep in and the shocking way that people carried on, taking their milk bottles in too soon and keeping cats.

Belladonna sighed. She could cope with one bluetit in her hair, but a whole family always gave her a headache.

"You can stay, but in my straw basket," she said, managing for once to be firm.

Doris, fortunately, was still asleep, her body bleached

to the whiteness of the bath, her vile eyes peacefully closed. Belladonna cleaned her teeth and went downstairs. The rooms were deserted and silent still. She didn't feel like the other witches this morning; she didn't feel like anybody. And slipping out of a side door into the street, she began to walk away from the hotel.

She walked and she walked and she walked, letting her feet carry her where they would, and presently she found that she had left the pleasant gardens and smart shops which surrounded the Grand Spa Hotel and was in a poor and slummy part of the town where the houses were neglected and dirty, orange peel and broken glass littered the gutters, and mangy dogs foraged in the dustbins.

She crossed a mean little square with a few dusty laurel bushes, a boarded-up lemonade stall, and a public lavatory, and found herself in front of a large, gray building with curtains the color of bile. A flight of mottled stone steps led from the side of the building into a patch of gravel and scuffed earth which might once have been a garden. And there, hunched on the low wall which ran beside the pavement, was a small boy. He was looking down at something that he held cupped in his skinny hands and making that kind of hiccuping noise that people make when they are trying not to cry.

What was cupped in the boy's hands was an earthworm. And the name of the boy—a name he hated—was Terence Mugg.

When he was a very small baby, Terence Mugg had been found wrapped in a newspaper in a telephone kiosk behind the railway station. The newspaper had smelt of vinegar, and the lady who found it had thought at first that it was a packet of fish and chips. However, when the fish and chips packet burst and put out a small, pink hand, she screamed and ran for a policeman.

At the police station, Terence was fed and clothed and photographed in the arms of a pretty policewoman. But when his picture appeared in the paper no one said, "Ooh!" and "Aah!" and "Isn't he sweet?," and no one wrote in offering to adopt him (though an old gentleman wrote in offering to adopt the policewoman). Terence just wasn't that kind of baby. There were even people cruel enough to say they might have left him in a telephone kiosk themselves.

So poor Terence was sent to the Sunnydene Children's Home in the most dismal part of Todcaster, and Matron christened him "Terence" after an actor she fancied at the time and "Mugg" because she said, "With a mug like that, what else can he be called?"

Babies in children's homes usually get adopted quite

quickly, but not Terence. Not only was he an unusually plain baby, but he spent the first five years of his life getting not only chicken pox and whooping cough, but really quite unusual things like brain fever and dermatitis and croup. Naturally nobody wants to adopt a baby whose entire head is swathed in bandages or whose face is covered with spots or who can't digest cheese without turning as yellow as a lentil. By the time he was five and had started at the local school, Terence had quite given up hope of finding a family to love him.

"We'll have *that* one with us for life," Matron would say nastily as Terence crept past her like a battered little snail. "No Mrs. Right's going to come along for *him*."

People who are lonely and unloved often turn to animals for company, and that was what Terence had done. Only, of course, at the Sunnydene Children's Home, Matron did not allow proper pets. So it was little things—small spiders and hurrying wood lice and shiny beetles—that Terence played with when he was out in the waste patch they called a garden, or found under paving stones on the way to school.

It was in this way that he had found Rover.

Rover was an earthworm, a pale pink, slender animal with a mauve bulge in the middle, a pointed end, and a peaceful way of crawling along the ground.

Terence had liked him immediately. There was something a little special about Rover. He did not seem quite like other worms, who often appear to have no notion of doing anything beyond burrowing down into the soil. Rover would curl into knots around Terence's fingers or lie quietly in the palm of his hand, and sometimes he would rear up his pointed end in a most intelligent way. Terence had found him in a tub of earth outside a chemist's shop, and he'd sneaked him into the home and found a place for him in the garden—a jam jar filled with leaf mold which he was careful to keep damp because his teacher had told him that earthworms breathe through their skins and should never get dry. He'd buried the jam jar behind a pile of bricks and told no one—only Billy, who was deaf and hadn't been adopted either. Billy was another person who didn't bother living things.

And there Rover had lived as happily as anything until last night when Matron had found Terence and Billy talking to him when they should have been inside getting ready for bed.

"How *dare* you!" she had shouted, charging down the garden like an ill-tempered camel. "Come inside at once! And throw that disgusting, unsanitary worm away immediately!"

And when Terence did not instantly do what he was told, she snatched Rover's jar and turned it upside down, scuffing at the leaf mold with her sharp and spiky shoes.

She had hurt Rover. hurt him badly. He was no better this morning: there was a wound in his middle where the skin was broken and his insides were spilling out in a terrible way. Rover wasn't moving, either; he just lay there, perfectly still and stretched in Terence's hand.

He was going to die.

"Hallo!" said a soft and musical voice above his head, and Terence, looking up, saw the most beautiful girl he had ever seen—a girl he would have been frightened of except that her blue eyes looked sad, and sadness was something Terence knew about. "My name is Belladonna," the gentle voice went on. "What's yours?"

The little boy flushed. "Terence Mugg," he said, staring up at her through his big, steel-rimmed spectacles. "And this," he swallowed, "is Rover. Only," he said, keeping his voice steady with an effort, "I think he's going . . . to die."

Belladonna looked carefully at the worm. She did not think Rover was an odd name for an earthworm.

She knew at once that he was called Rover because Terence dreadfully wanted a dog and knew he would never get one. And she knew, too, that Terence was right about Rover. The worm was very, very sick.

"May I hold him for a moment?" she asked.

Terence hesitated. When somebody that belongs to you is going to die you feel you should hold on to him and help him right to the end. But when he saw the look on Belladonna's face he carefully opened his hand and gave her his worm.

Belladonna bent over Rover and her hair fell like a golden curtain, inside which the wounded worm lay snug and warm. Then she began to croon a little song.

Terence had never heard a song like the one that Belladonna sang. It was about dampness and the soft darkness of the rich earth and about the patient worms who had turned it through the years. It was a song about pinkness and wetness and roundness, and while she sang it, Terence felt that he, too, was an earthworm and understood the soul of all earthworms and always would. Then she blew three times on her cupped hands and parted them.

"Let's see now," she said.

"Oh!" said Terence. *"Oh!"*

The little jagged place where Matron's shoe had hit the earthworm's side was quite closed over. Rover's skin was smooth again, there was no scar, and even as

Terence gazed at him, Rover reared up his pointed end in just the jaunty way he used to.

Terence was possibly the ugliest little boy that Belladonna had ever seen, but now his face was shining like an archangel's. "He's better! He's all right again! You *healed* him! Oh, Rover, you're fine again, you're better than before!" He looked up at Belladonna. "Only you didn't give him any medicine or anything. Are you a vet, then?" But his face was puzzled because he had seen vets and they did not look like Belladonna.

"Well, not exactly," said Belladonna. "But sometimes I can—" She broke off and flinched. Quite the most unpleasant voice she had ever heard was coming at her from the top of the steps.

"Where is that dratted boy," it whined. "Skulking in the garden again! Really, I don't know why they bothered to fish him out of the telephone kiosk, he's been nothing but trouble since the day he arrived."

The unpleasant voice belonged to a tall, bony woman with a yellowish skin and a nose you could have cut cheese with.

"It's Matron," whispered Terence as he drew closer to Belladonna.

"Oh, there you are, you wretched boy! Well, come in at *once* or you'll have no lunch. And if you've still got that slimy worm I'm going to flush him down the lavatory, and you after him!"

She began to charge down the steps, and Belladonna could feel Terence shrinking beside her. "No,"
he said. "Please. I'll put him away."

Matron took no notice at all. She had reached the
bottom step and was coming at them along the gravel
path. "As for you," she said, glaring at Belladonna,
"I'd like to know what you're doing, trespassing in a
private garden."

"Will you take him?" Terence whispered.

Belladonna nodded and slipped Rover into her
hand. Then she put her arm round Terence's shoulders. And as she felt the shivers that shook his thin little frame, a great anger shot through her. Belladonna
was almost never angry, but she was angry now. Very
angry.

Belladonna closed her eyes. She took a deep breath.
And then she called on a god that white witches do not
usually call on. "Oh, great Cernunnos, you horned
one, please help me halt this *revolting* woman!"

Matron was coming closer. Closer still . . . Then
suddenly she stumbled and looked back at her left
foot. She tugged at it. She pulled. Nothing happened.
Matron's left foot would not move.

"Oh!" gasped Terence. *"Look!"*

A little bulge had appeared at the tip of Matron's
left shoe. Then the leather burst open and a green
root appeared and began to snake along the ground

and bury itself in the soil. From the side of the shoe came another root, and another. . . . The roots grew thicker and stronger; gnarled they were now, like the roots of an ancient beech and always pushing down, down into the ground.

"Help!" shrieked Matron. "Help! *Eek!*"

It was happening to the other foot now. From her heels, her toes, her ankles, her knobbly knees . . . Roots that began soft and green and became thicker and more twisted as they grew downward; roots like great creepers, like ropes—and all tethering Matron as if with bands of steel to the ground.

"Help!" shrieked Matron again. But no one heard her, and now the roots were coming out of her waist, her arms. . . . And then she could shriek no more because a tendril had sprung out of her upper lip and was snaking down toward the ground, closing her mouth as firmly as a trap.

"*Oh!*" said Terence once again. He was still nestling against her skirt, but when Belladonna looked down she saw that he wasn't frightened, just amazed. "You did it!" said Terence, "I know you did it. You're magic, aren't you? You're a witch!"

Belladonna nodded. She, too, was very much excited, because rooting people to the ground is magic all right, but it is not really very white. Rooting a begonia or a cabbage or a clump of wallflowers is white

because begonias and cabbages and clumps of wall-flowers like to have roots and cannot live without them. But rooting matrons is a different matter. If it wasn't actually *black* magic, it was certainly fairly gray, and Belladonna's eyes were shining as she looked at Terence.

"You've brought me luck," she said. "You and Rover. That's the blackest thing I've done, *ever.*"

"You mean you usually do white magic, like healing people and so on?" said Terence. It struck Belladonna that he seemed to have a natural feeling for magic and not to show any of the fears one would expect in so nervous a boy. "But do you *want* to be black?"

"Yes, I do. I do terribly," said Belladonna. And she explained about the competition and Arriman. She was too shy to tell Terence that she loved Arriman, but she thought he had probably guessed. He was that kind of little boy. Suddenly a thought struck her. "Terence, you don't think . . ." She looked down at the worm, now distinctly perky and inclined to tie himself into knots around her finger. "You don't think that Rover . . . that he might be a *familiar.* I never had one, you know. The other witches did, but I didn't. Do you think"—Belladonna was growing very excited now—"do you think it was because I was holding Rover that I managed to root Matron?"

"It might be." Terence was as excited as she was.

"Only I thought familiars were usually black cats and hares and goats and things?"

"Oh, no." And Belladonna explained about the octopus called Doris, and Madame Olympia's aardvark, and the cloud of flies.

"He's so little," said Terence. There was a pause, broken only by a furious, suffocated grunt from Matron, up whose legs a large black spider was steadily marching. "But if he has helped you," Terence went on bravely, "then you must have him. Take him with you so's you win the competition."

Belladonna was incredibly touched.

"I couldn't, Terence. I couldn't separate you two. You belong together. Anyway, I haven't a hope of winning the competition even so."

But Terence now was clutching her arm and looking up at her, his eyes pleading.

"If you couldn't separate us, couldn't you . . . Oh, please, *please* couldn't you take me with you? Witches have servants, I know they do. Imps and . . . fiends and things. I'd do anything for you, *anything.*"

"Oh, Terence, I'd love to, but how can I? I'm staying in this posh hotel and they'd never let you come. And anyway, witches don't really mix with ordinary people, you know. It never comes right."

But her voice trailed away as she said it, for what was "right" for Terence about the Sunnydene Children's

Home? And what would happen to him when Matron stopped being rooted? Belladonna had absolutely no idea how long the spell would last, and the glitter in Matron's eye as she tugged uselessly at her roots boded extremely ill for Terence.

Terence did not say anything. He just stood there, dejected and beaten, but still holding out his worm to her.

"Oh, heck," said Belladonna suddenly, making up her mind. "Let's just *do* it. It may come right."

She climbed over the low wall and turned, stretching out a hand to Terence. Then, followed by the strangled grunts of the rooted Matron, they ran together down the road.

CHAPTER 6

WHEN BELLADONNA GOT BACK to the hotel, she took Terence straight to the manager's office to see Mr. Leadbetter and the ogre.

She found them in a bad way. There had been a row about Ethel Feedbag's pig, which was not house-trained, and when the manager complained, Ethel (who had not been well brought up) said: "Oh, go and teach your grandmother to suck eggs!" Unfortunately, she had been clutching her hazel wand at the time and the next moment the manager found himself in a nursing home in Bexhill-on-Sea holding out a raw egg to his mother's mother, a frail old lady who had been looking forward to her morning porridge and was very much annoyed.

The muddle had taken a long time to clear up, and then it was discovered that Mother Bloodwort, who had been riding up and down in the hotel lift all morning, had got jammed between floors. Trying to remember the spell for making things go up in the air, she had got mixed up and become a coffee table once again, and since coffee tables cannot press emergency buttons, she had caused a great deal of trouble to the engineers.

But when they saw Belladonna, the secretary and the ogre both cheered up and greeted Terence most politely.

Belladonna lost no time in explaining about Terence and the horrible home. "And he's brought this absolutely *marvelous* familiar!" she went on. "He made me able to do a really quite black thing. Me!"

The ogre and Mr. Leadbetter looked around the room, wondering if they had missed a stampeding bufflalo or a wolverine with slavering fangs, but all they could see was a small and skinny boy, his gaze fixed wonderingly on the ogre's single eye.

"Show them, Terence," said Belladonna.

So Terence felt in his pocket and lifted out Rover and put him carefully down on Mr. Leadbetter's blotter. The secretary and the ogre bent over him and their hearts sank—a small, pale worm whose bristles, as he crawled across the paper, made a delicate soughing noise like autumn leaves stirred by the softest of winds. And for a moment they'd really hoped!

"Shall I try the typewriter?" Belladonna asked eagerly. "Like you wanted me to yesterday? A nest of vipers, wasn't it? Come on, Terence."

So Terence picked up Rover and stood beside her, and Belladonna rested her fingertips lightly on the little worm's mauve and slightly bulgy middle and closed her eyes. And, lo and behold, the typewriter vanished with a puff and there on the desk was a writhing mass of hissing vipers with darting tongues and slitty, yellow eyes.

"Poor little things," said Belladonna, forgetting her blackness for a moment. "They look awfully dry."

"Vipers is born dry," said Lester, "so don't you go fretting yourself."

But the look he exchanged with Mr. Leadbetter was eager and excited. If Belladonna could get black so quickly, there was hope yet!

"Amazing!" said Mr. Leadbetter. He looked at Rover again to see if he had missed anything: a hidden poison sac, a lethal sting—but the worm now crawling peaceably up Terence's sleeve was exactly what he seemed: gentle, modest, and moist.

"So, I was wondering," said Belladonna, putting her arm around Terence's shoulder, "if Terence could *possibly* stay for a bit? Rover belongs to him, and though he offered to give him to me, I just *couldn't* take him away."

Mr. Leadbetter looked worried. What would the manager say to another guest? And what about the other witches? Would it start an absolute avalanche of witch friends and relations coming to stay at the hotel? Fishy little Wracks and quarreling Shouter cousins and small Feedbags in nasty Wellington boots?

Terence said nothing. He just stood there, waiting. He was not a boy who had ever hoped for much.

Mr. Leadbetter cleared his throat. "It so happens," he began, "that I have a sister. Amelia, her name is. Amelia Leadbetter."

The ogre and Belladonna looked at him anxiously. They knew how hard he had been working and that overwork can drive people a little mad.

"She didn't, in fact, marry," Mr. Leadbetter went on. "But she might have done. There was a swimming bath attendant who was very fond of her."

The others waited.

"I'm not saying that the swimming bath attendant was called Mugg," the secretary went on, "because he wasn't. His name, actually, was Arthur Hurtleypool. I remember it because jokes were made about hurtleying into the pool, that kind of thing. Still, if he *had* been called Mugg and if he had married my sister Amelia and if the marriage had been blessed with a son, then this son," finished the secretary, "would undoubtedly have been my nephew."

"Your nephew, Terence!" said Belladonna, seeing the light.

"Precisely. And what more natural than that my sister, Amelia, having to go into the hospital to have her appendix out, should send Terence to stay with me?"

"Oh, Mr. Leadbetter, you're wonderful," cried Belladonna, throwing her arms around the secretary, a thing he very much enjoyed.

Terence looked as though he'd swallowed a lighted candle. But when he spoke it was to say haltingly: "If I was your nephew, shouldn't I have . . ." He was too shy to finish, but his eyes went to the back of Mr. Leadbetter and lingered there. The secretary was a modest man, so much so that he usually wore his stump inside his trousers, but Terence was a boy who noticed things.

"A tail?" said Mr. Leadbetter.

Terence nodded.

"I could make him a little one," said Belladonna. "Even without Rover. Making tails is *growing* magic, and there's nothing whiter than that. But I don't know. . . . I feel Terence is sort of perfect as he is."

Terence looked up quickly. Surely Belladonna was mocking him? But no—her periwinkle eyes were very clear and very loving as she looked at him, and he had to turn away because a lump had come up in his throat.

"Quite honestly, Terence," said Mr. Leadbetter, "if

you *can* manage without one, it would be better. There is, you *see,* the problem of sitting down. And my sister Amelia—your mother, that would be—was perfectly tailless, as far as I recall."

Terence didn't keep on about it after that. To be able to be near Belladonna, to know that *his* worm might help her to gain her heart's desire, was happiness enough. Only someone really greedy and undisciplined would also expect a tail.

"I'll tell you one thing, though," said Lester. "I wouldn't say anything about Rover being such a powerful familiar. I'd let Terence look after Rover and pretend he was just a pet, that's what I'd do. If it gets around that Rover's giving Belladonna even half a chance of winning the competition, I wouldn't give a fig for *his* chances."

"Oh, no, *surely,* no one would hurt an innocent worm like that!" said Belladonna.

"Now, Belladonna, try *thinking* black as well as acting it. There's already been some hanky-panky with Doris. Lurching about the bath she was, drunk as a lord and a nasty pea green color with it—and Ms. Wrack saying Doris never touched a drop and someone must have forced it down her throat."

"Oh, *poor* Doris—is she all right now?" cried Belladonna.

"Well, it seems she'd been on the bath salts. But it

just shows," said Lester darkly. "I wouldn't trust any of those witches as far as I could throw them, let alone that Madame Olympia."

A chill spread round the room as they remembered the enchantress's cruel smile and the necklace of human teeth.

"And what about those Shouter chickens? You know how they follow you about. One peck at Rover and you'll be back to bloomin' begonias," the ogre went on.

Belladonna saw the sense of this. "They wouldn't *mean* to, of course; they'd feel dreadful afterward, but all the same . . ." She turned to Terence. "All right, you shall be Rover's *bodyguard* and keep him, and when I want to do some magic you can come over and stand beside me and I'll touch Rover without anyone seeing."

"That's the ticket," said the ogre.

It was decided that Terence should sleep on a camp bed in Mr. Leadbetter's room and make himself useful generally until it was time to go to Darkington, and when Belladonna had turned the vipers back into a typewriter again, she and Terence went to wash their hands for lunch.

In the afternoon, Mr. Leadbetter took the witches to a big department store called Turnbull and Buttle to buy the long, black gowns and hoods that they were to wear for the competition. He had hoped to have Lester to help him, but Arriman had sent for the ogre, spiriting him away just as he was about to lift a spoonful of banana fritter to his mouth, and it was Mr. Leadbetter alone who had to shepherd the witches up to the third floor and stop Mabel Wrack from leaping onto the fish slab and return the cigarettes that had mysteriously flown through the air into the handbags of the Shouter twins and explain to the young man behind the glove counter that he couldn't immediately marry Belladonna.

Fortunately the gowns were waiting for them: black ones with hoods like schoolteachers used to wear, and long enough to reach right down to the ground and cover Mother Bloodwort's slippers and Ethel Feedbag's Wellies, so that with the black carnival masks that Turnbull and Buttle had ordered specially, there really was no way of telling which witch was which.

But when it came to Madame Olympia's turn to try on her gown, she made a nasty scene. All day, the enchantress had kept snootily to her room, insisting that meals be sent up to her, ordering incredible delicacies for the aardvark, and putting out seventeen pairs of shoes for the poor boot boy to clean.

Now she looked at her plain cotton gown and said:

"Are you out of your *mind*? Do you imagine I can perform magic in that *rag*!"

"I'm afraid all the witches have to be dressed alike," said Mr. Leadbetter. "It's one of the rules of the competition."

"Then the rules must be broken," said the enchantress, fixing Mr. Leadbetter with an evil and glittering eye.

It is impossible to say what would have happened next, but just at that moment Mother Bloodwort, who had been resting on a low gilt chair, gave a shriek of excitement.

"It's me toe! Me big toe! It's happened. I can feel it!"

Belladonna put down her gown and hurried over to her. "What has, Mother Bloodwort?"

"It's my turning-myself-young-again spell! I've been working on it all week, and just now me big toe gave this splutter. More of a *spurt* it was, really. Like a spring chicken it felt, rarin' to go."

She began to scrabble under her musty skirt, removed her stockings, shook off a couple of the small, gray bandages which clung like dead mice around her ankles, and stuck her naked foot into the air.

The stunned shop assistants drew closer; the witches clustered around.

"It is . . . *pinker* than the others, I'm almost sure," said Belladonna at last. "And sort of . . . fuller-looking."

"Rubbish," said Nancy Shouter. "It's exactly like the others and nasty with it."

"You've made the whole thing up," said Mabel Wrack, pursing her codlike lips.

"And your toenails need cutting."

The unkind remarks of the other witches came thick and fast. And it had to be admitted that Mother Bloodwort's toe did look exactly like all the others: yellow and bent with little tufty hairs.

But Mother Bloodwort was not to be put down. "You'll see one day, all of you. When I get the rest of the spell, you'll see, I'll be so young you'll have to put me into nappies!"

But she allowed Belladonna to help her on with her stockings and lead her back to the bus. It had been rather an exciting day.

When Lester found himself spirited away to Darkington in the middle of his banana fritter, he had a feeling that his master was up to no good, and he was right. Arriman had sent for him to tell him that the witches couldn't stay at the hall during the competition.

"But sir—" began Lester.

Arriman, who was in his library, waved a hand.

"Don't try to persuade me, Lester. Even if they stay in the east wing as you suggested, even if they're completely covered in their hoods and gowns, I just can't face it."

Lester tried not to show it, but he was annoyed. It seemed to him that Arriman was doing everything he could to make the contest as difficult as possible. After all, if you wanted a black witch, what was the use of fussing about a few warts with whiskers on them or a sea slug over someone's eye? For a moment, he wondered whether to mention Madame Olympia. Arriman hadn't seen her yet and she might be more his type. About Belladonna he decided to say nothing. The disappointment if she didn't win would be bad enough without raising any hopes.

"Well, where are they to stay, then?" he asked.

Arriman brightened. "I had a good idea. I want them to camp in the west meadow, the one opposite the main gate. They'll be out of the way there. Just buy everything you need—those pretty orange tents with little plastic porches and camp stoves and those cunning canvas lavatories. Buy everything," he said grandly, "and send the bill to me."

"But it's October, sir! They'll be freezing!"

"No, no—not at all. Braced is what they'll be. Toned up. Those nylon sleeping bags are very good, I hear. You'll have to excuse me now, Lester—I have the judges arriving tonight."

As he came away from the library, Lester met the Wizard Watcher.

"How do you find him?" asked the Left Head.

79

"Off his chump," said the ogre. "Wants the witches to camp in the west meadow. Won't have them in the house."

The monster sighed. "He's taken it hard," said the Middle Head. "You can imagine how we feel, letting him down."

"Still, if the wizard didn't cometh, what could we do?" remarked the Left Head.

"And cometh he definitely didn't," the Right Head said.

The monster then told Lester that it had asked for a holiday during the actual contest. It was just going to take a rucksack and go walkabout.

"We'll be back for the wedding, of course," said the Middle Head. "But everyone'll be better for a break."

Lester nodded. He could see that, in spite of itself, the Wizard Watcher felt it had somehow failed in its task and wanted to be alone till it felt better.

"What's with Sir Simon?" he said. "Seems to me the old man's seeing a bit too much of him, eh?"

He had no sooner spoken than there was a moaning sound, followed by the clank of leg armor and the hollow, gloomy specter of the wife-slayer passed through them in the corridor.

"Gone to watch the old man noshing," said the Middle Head disapprovingly.

"Thick as thieves, they are," said the Left Head.

"Gets me down, all that beating his blinking forehead," complained the Right Head. "I mean, if you've murdered your wives, you've murdered them and that's *it*."

Lester's great craggy brow was so furrowed that the eye patch seemed to be riding a storm-tossed sea.

"I don't like it," he said. "There's something fishy going on between those two, you mark my words."

He sighed and pulled a saber out of the umbrella stand. There was never anything decent to swallow at the hotel.

"Ready, sir," he called upstairs to Arriman.

And with a whoosh, he was gone.

CHAPTER 7

*T*HE NEWS THAT the witches were to camp hit Mr. Leadbetter extremely hard. Once, before he came to work for Arriman, he had taken a camping holiday in the south of France. He could remember a huge ironmonger's daughter from Berlin who had lost her way back to her tent at night and fallen like a felled ox across his guy ropes. He could remember an old Greek lady cutting her toenails into the sinks, and three sunburnt Italian men who had stumped up and down with blaring transistors. He remembered the dead toad caught in the slatted floor of the shower block and the hairy housewife from Luxembourg who had sat on the steps of her caravan shaving her legs. And when he remembered that these were *ordinary* people, the thought of what the witches would make of camping made him groan aloud. "Sometimes I don't know what

I've done to deserve it, Lester, honestly I don't," he said to the ogre.

But of course he went out, good secretary that he was, and ordered everything he could think of: tents and sleeping bags and folding chairs, and had the stuff sent up to Darkington. Then he borrowed the manager's top hat and wrote the numbers one to seven on bits of paper and put them inside the hat and left it on the piano stool in the ballroom ready for the witches to draw lots on the following day for their place in the contest.

"Perhaps Madame Olympia would care to draw first?" he suggested, when he had gathered them together after breakfast.

So the enchantress, dragging her aardvark by his rhinestone collar, came forward and put her hand into the hat.

"Is this some sort of joke?" she said disdainfully, putting the thing she had just pulled out onto the piano stool.

It was an egg.

There was only the shortest of pauses and then it began: "That is an egg laid by *my* chicken," said Nancy Shouter.

"Oh, no it isn't. That is an egg laid by *my* chicken. I could tell that egg anywhere."

The other witches came closer. There is always excitement when a familiar lays an egg. There could so easily be a small dragon inside or a dark stain which could be trained to grow up into a fiend—anything— and for once they could see what the Shouter twins were quarreling about.

Mr. Leadbetter sighed. He did so want to get on with drawing lots.

Ethel Feedbag now stepped forward. Working at the egg packing station, she was reckoned to be an expert.

"That egg," she pronounced, "be, simply—an egg."

This, of course, set the Shouters off again.

"How *dare* you suggest that *my* chicken could lay an ordinary egg."

"Not your chicken! *My* chicken!"

Ethel shrugged. Nancy Shouter picked up the egg. Nora Shouter tried to pull it away from her. The next second they were all peering down at the mess of yellow yolk, transparent white, and bits of shell sploshed across the carpet.

Ethel was perfectly right. Whichever of the chickens had laid it, the thing was simply an egg.

When at last they got round to drawing lots it worked out like this: Mabel Wrack was number one, which meant that she would be the first to do her trick, Ethel Feedbag was number two, and the Shouter twins had drawn three and four. Mother Bloodwort was number five, and Madame Olympia was number six. And the witch who would do her trick last, on the actual night of Halloween, and who had drawn number seven—was Belladonna.

"Fine Halloween that'll be," sneered Nancy Shouter. "Blinking nightingales all over the place and angels singing the Hallelujah Chorus, I shouldn't wonder."

Once, those words would have hurt Belladonna badly, but not now. Only half an hour earlier, with Rover and Terence, she had turned the ashtray in her bedroom into a hideous, grinning skull.

There was only one more thing for the witches to do, and in a way it was the most important of all. They had to decide on which piece of magic they were going to do and make lists of all the things they needed for it so that they could be got ready and waiting for them at the hall. All the other witches seemed to know—you could hear them plotting and whispering and hiding bits of paper from each other all over the hotel—but not Belladonna. Being black needs a lot of practice and a completely different way of thinking to being white, and when she tried to imagine a trick foul and vicious enough to please Arriman, her mind just went completely blank.

"Oh, Terence, I *wish* I knew what to do," she said to the little boy who was sitting beside her on the bed.

Even in the two days since he had left the home, Terence seemed to have changed. His mud-colored eyes had grown bright and eager, his hair was no longer plastered to his head but bounced with life, and he wore his spectacles at quite a jaunty angle on the end of his nose. Happiness is almost as good as magic for altering a person's looks.

"I suppose Mabel Wrack will do some watery, fishy kind of trick," Belladonna went on. "And Ethel Feedbag's sure to do something countryish, and Madame Olympia . . ." But the thought of Madame Olympia's trick was horrible in a special sort of way, and Belladonna left her sentence unfinished.

She picked up the mirror. Arriman was playing solitaire—not cheating exactly but sometimes rearranging the cards a little. The look on his dark, brooding face, the white hair in his curse curl, made her heart turn over. She was just going to put the mirror down again when a gray, wavering shape passed over its surface, and she saw Arriman look up eagerly.

"Is that Sir Simon?" asked Terence. It was his first sight of the wicked specter.

Belladonna nodded. "He's his special friend."

"Why is he banging at his forehead like that?" Terence wanted to know.

"It's guilt. Because he killed all his wives. It makes a

plashing noise, Lester says, but we can't hear it because the mirror's silent."

"Is that all he does?" Terence asked. "Can't he speak or anything?"

Belladonna shook her head. "You've got to remember he's been dead for four hundred years. Whatever it is people speak with must have got very withered up by now." She sighed. "It must be so *lonely* for Arriman, having a friend who can't say anything. I mean, a plashing sound is not the same."

Suddenly Terence gave a little cry and Belladonna saw that behind his spectacles his bright, mud-colored eyes were positively sparkling with excitement.

"Belladonna, I've had a *marvelous* idea! For your trick. Why don't you raise Sir Simon? Bring him back to life?"

Belladonna stared at him. "Terence, I *couldn't*. Not *possibly*. That's the blackest magic in the whole world. Witches didn't just get burnt at the stake for that; they got hung and drawn and quartered and rolled up into little balls of *dung*."

Terence didn't seem to think this mattered. "But you want to be black, don't you? What's the point of being just a little bit black? If you're going to win, surely you have to do the most awful thing there is?"

"Yes, but I'd never *do* it. Arriman hasn't been

able to do it, and Lester says he's tried and tried and tried."

"Arriman hasn't got Rover," said Terence.

Belladonna was silent. The little boy's faith in his worm was somehow catching.

"Oh, Terence, do you really think I could?"

"Of *course* you could. And think how happy you'd be making Arriman. That's what you want when you love someone, isn't it? To make them happy?"

So he *had* guessed her secret.

"Yes," said Belladonna quietly, "that's what you want."

She got up and went over to the wooden box that Terence had fitted out for Rover to live in when he wasn't in the matchbox in his pocket. Just to know that the worm was there, cradled deep in layers of damp, rich earth, made her feel at once more evil, more wicked, and more dark.

"What shall I put on my list, then? There are awful things you need for necromancy. Warm sheep's blood, I think and . . . *pits* . . . and things."

Terence considered. "I wouldn't bother with all that," he said. "I think all that stuff's just for people who haven't got Rover. I reckon you've just got to *think* black."

So Belladonna got a sheet of hotel note paper out of the bureau and wrote, *Witch Number Seven: Nothing*, and went downstairs to give it to the secretary and the ogre.

Mr. Leadbetter had just finished reading the lists handed in by the other six witches, after which he had done something most unusual. He had sat down. Not even the pain as his stump grated against the seat could keep him on his feet. He had expected the witches to want a few things like crucibles and thuribles (whatever they were), a bit of wax for making images, perhaps a spot of moonwort or of mercury—that kind of thing. But no; the witches had really gone to town.

"Seven princesses!" cried Mr. Leadbetter, holding up the list that the chambermaid had written out for witch number five. "What does she think I am?"

Lester pulled skillfully at the handle of the saber sticking from his mouth and drew it from his gullet.

"These'll have to go up to the hall," he said, coming to stand behind the secretary. "We'll get the easy stuff, but the old man'll have to magic up the rest on the day. *I'm* not going into Turnbull and Buttle's to ask for seven princesses of the blood royal, nor are you."

Mr. Leadbetter nodded. Much as he hated failing Arriman, he could see that Lester was right.

It was just then that Belladonna knocked and slipped in quietly with her list.

"The dear girl," said Mr. Leadbetter when he'd read it. "She's never any trouble."

But secretly, the ogre and the secretary were anxious and dismayed. Did it mean that Belladonna had gone white again? That she wasn't even going to try? What kind of magic could one do with *nothing*?

Meanwhile, at Darkington Hall, the visiting judges had arrived.

When the competition had first been suggested, Arriman had thought of having a whole panel of judges as they do for the Miss World contest or the Olympic Games. But people who really knew about magic were getting hard to find, and anyway now that he had *seen* some of the witches, Arriman felt so gloomy that he just wanted to get everything over in the simplest way possible. He had written to a lady called The Hag of the Dribble to ask if she would come and be a judge, but she hadn't answered—probably there wasn't any writing paper in Dribble—and what he was left with was an extremely old, rather frail ghoul called Henry Sniveler and a genie called Mr. Chatterjee.

Mr. Chatterjee, like most genies, lived in a bottle out of which he swooshed if someone said the right words and remembered to unscrew the top. He was an Indian genie and felt the cold so dreadfully that mostly he liked to stay inside the bottle and talk through the

glass. As his accent was rather strong, this made it difficult to understand him, but he was a very fine judge of magic, having lived so long in the East, where they do a lot of interesting things like sending people up on flying carpets and then bringing them down suddenly so that their behinds become impaled on spikes.

Mr. Sniveler was a very different sort of person: a dark-faced, silent ghoul who lived behind a slaughter-house in a satanic northern town and spent the night foraging in dustbins for unspeakable, bloodred things, some of which he ate and some of which he collected. Ghouls are not particularly good at magic, but there is nothing darker, gloomier, or more evil than a ghoul, and Arriman knew that he had been very lucky to get him.

So now the three of them sat at dinner around the carved oak table in the great hall, where the firelight flickered, the ravens croaked in the rafters, and, on a rug, the weary Wizard Watcher rested its head. Arriman was in low spirits—the witches were due to arrive in a couple of days—and kind Mr. Chatterjee, who was dining inside his bottle because of the drafts, was doing his best to cheer him up.

"Oh, my goodness, it will not be so bad, I think, to have a wife," he said in his soft voice, sucking up a piece of spaghetti which Arriman had dropped in for him. Although tiny, he was most beautifully dressed in a white turban and a scarlet tunic frogged with gold.

The ghoul did not see it like that. "Yak!" he said. And presently, when he had swallowed a fish finger: "Ugh."

Arriman was just beginning to explain about the contest and how it should be judged when there was the usual plashing and moaning and Sir Simon appeared through the tapestry and thrust his pale and ghastly face at Arriman.

"You see," said the wizard gloomily. "He's trying to warn me. Seven times he's been married and each time his wife drove him to murder. Quite simply *drove* him."

"Oh, dearie me!" said Mr. Chatterjee, very much upset. "How has he been murdering so many, please?"

Arriman shrugged. "The usual methods, I suppose. Drowning, stabbing, strangulation—that kind of thing."

"Then it is good he is only a ghost," said the little genie, "or your new wife will perhaps be number eight."

Arriman threw him a sharp look from beneath his dev- ilish eyebrows. "It's only his *own* wives he kills," he said. But for a while he stared abstractedly into the fire as though turning a new and important idea over in his mind.

"Well now, gentlemen," he said at last. "To busi- ness. I thought each witch should be given ten points. Two for darkness, two for power, two for presenta- tion. . ."

There was a swoosh and Mr. Chatterjee came out of his bottle, growing almost to normal size as he did. Like most genies, he was very serious about his work.

And for the next hour, while the shadows length- ened and the Wizard Watcher slept, the judges of the Miss Witch of Todcaster contest bent over their task.

CHAPTER 8

*T*HE WITCHES' CAMPING wasn't as bad as Mr. Leadbetter had thought it would be. It was worse.

Not that there was anything wrong with the campsite. The campsite was very nice. Mr. Leadbetter had ordered a caravan for Mother Bloodwort, who had seemed to him too old to do well under canvas, and tents and a toilet block with showers and absolutely the latest kind of chemical loo. But the witches hadn't been in the west meadow for twenty-four hours before pandemonium set in.

For a start, Mother Bloodwort never got into her caravan at all. Madame Olympia nabbed it straightaway, no one knew how, and sat inside it with the aardvark, despising the other witches and refusing to take her turn at any of the chores. Nancy and Nora Shouter spent the first night quarreling about which of them had the better camp bed and ended by sticking penknives into each other's air mattresses. Ethel Feedbag's pig escaped from its pen and crashed into Mother Bloodwort's tent, sending the old witch flying just as she was trying to fix a mouse-blood poultice under her nightdress, and Mabel Wrack insisted on using the cooking cauldron to give Doris a bubble bath, which made the breakfast porridge taste very strange indeed.

It was Belladonna, of course, who was left to fetch the water and do the cooking and the washing up, and however hard she tried to please everybody—braising cod's eyes for Mabel Wrack and roasting squashed hedgehogs on hot bricks for Ethel Feedbag—she got nothing but grumbles and sneers for her pains.

And Belladonna had her own troubles. Mr. Leadbetter and the ogre were back in their old rooms up at the hall, and as Terence was supposed to be Mr. Leadbetter's nephew, he had been given a little room beside the secretary's in the servants' wing. This meant that Rover, too, was far away at the end of the long drive, sleeping in his wooden box under Terence's window. And with her familiar out of reach, Belladonna's old trouble was coming back, and coming back badly. The very first morning she had woken to find that her sleeping bag had come out in a rash of passionflowers— great, pollen-loaded things that tickled abominably and made her sneeze, and when she opened the flap of her tent she found six twitch-eared, bright-eyed baby rabbits waiting for her, their paws in the air.

"I'm not a white witch now, you know," she said crossly. But of course she let them in and conjured up a patch of lettuce for them out of her groundsheet, and it was clear to everybody that they were to stay.

But if life was hard on the camping site in the west meadow, it wasn't exactly easy at the hall. Mr. Sniveler, the ghoul, who was sleeping in the tapestry room, found it difficult to break the habit of years and spent the night scooping fungus off the cellar walls and filching raw mince from the refrigerator and taking them to bed. This meant that he was usually very tired during the day and fell asleep all over the place, waking up suddenly to say things like, "Blood!" or "Slime!" which made it difficult to carry on a sensible conversation. Poor Mr. Chatterjee had caught a cold and sat inside his bottle sneezing miserably so that the glass misted up and he couldn't see out. As for Arriman, well, as Lester said: "Anyone would think he was goin' to have his bloomin' head chopped off instead of getting hitched, the way he's carrying on."

In the bustle and fuss that led up to the start of the competition, Terence turned out to be worth his weight in gold. He ran errands, found the wizard's socks, removed the bits of bandage with scabs on them from Mr. Sniveler's bed, and stuffed Mr. Chatterjee's bottle with paper tissue so that the little genie could blow his swollen nose. And everything he did, he did happily and with delight because Darkington, with its devilish maze and stinking laboratory and ghastly zoo, seemed to him the most enchanting place in the whole world.

But what Terence did whenever he could be spared was to study Sir Simon Montpelier, and quite soon he knew as much about the wicked wife-slayer as Arriman himself. He learned that the specter usually appeared first in the broom cupboard, where he limbered up with a couple of groans, half a dozen eerie thumps, and a wail or two, before settling into the serious business of smiting his forehead with a plashing sound. Then, still plashing for all he was worth, the unhappy phantom would set off through the laundry room, up the stairs to the library, pass through a couple of bookcases and a stuffed bison, and end up in the great hall, popping out through a tapestry of a man being stuck full of arrows while being burnt at the stake, and ruining the appetite of whomever was at dinner.

"You'll see," said Terence to Belladonna, who was stirring the witches' supper over the campfire. "He'll be absolutely terrific when he's raised. When you get close to him, his face is all sort of loathsome and ruined-looking. When he bursts through the wall, *alive*, it'll be a sensation."

"Oh, Terence, I do hope so," said Belladonna. The baby rabbits hadn't gone, nor had the passionflowers, and the tree behind her tent was bearing golden pears. "Tell me," she went on, "how is he? Is he still so sad?"

She meant Arriman, of course. The great magician was seldom from her mind.

"Well, he is a bit. But you've got to remember that he's never seen you and that he doesn't know you're going to win."

"No," said Belladonna. "He certainly doesn't know *that.*"

But already she felt blacker and more hopeful. It was always like that when Terence came.

And so, at last, after all the preparations and the fuss, the first day of the contest dawned.

Mabel Wrack—witch number one—had got up early and stood for two hours under the shower so that her legs did not dry out on her big day. She had dressed with care, fastening the sea-slug brooch beneath her gown, but she was not nervous. Owing to Mrs. Wrack having been a mermaid, Mabel was one quarter fish and, as is well known, fishes are cold-blooded and never get excited.

As everyone had expected, Mabel had decided to do

her trick beside the sea. The place she had chosen was called the Devil's Cauldron: a sandy bay flanked by brooding granite cliffs and strewn with jagged rocks to which dark seaweed slimily clung.

Backing the sand was a strip of turf, and it was here, at a trestle table which Lester had dragged out for them, that the judges sat. Arriman the Awful, wearing his robe with the constellations on it, was in the middle; Mr. Chatterjee (inside his bottle on account of the nippy breeze) was on the magician's left, and on the right—pale and exhausted after a night of hideous wandering—dropped Mr. Sniveler. The other witches, gowned and masked so that Arriman couldn't catch even an accidental glimpse of them, were huddled behind a clump of gorse bushes—all except Madame Olympia, who had stayed snootily inside her caravan.

Arriman now got up to make a speech. He declared the Ms. Witch of Todcaster contest open and welcomed all the competitors. He reminded them of the rules—any witch practicing black magic on another witch or her familiars would be disqualified, the competitors must not show their faces, and the judges' decision was final. Then he sat down and Mr. Leadbetter, shouting through a megaphone like a film director, said:

"Witch number one—step forward!"

There was clapping from the other witches, and from some villagers who had come up the cliff path, and Mabel emerged from behind the gorse bushes. Only the lower part of her face showed beneath the mask, but it was enough to make Arriman hope frantically that she was going to go to sea in a sieve and drown.

"Present your list!" ordered Mr. Leadbetter, and Mabel went up to the judges' table with her piece of paper. In the neat hand of a practiced shopkeeper, Mabel had written:

1. *One gong (loud)*
2. *Some golden rings*
3. *A drowned sailor*

"The manager of the hotel was kind enough to lend us his gong," said Mr. Leadbetter. "And we got the golden rings from Woolworth's. But there is this matter of the drowned sailor."

"Hm," said Arriman, looking rather sick. There is a place called Davy Jones's locker under the sea, where the bodies of drowned sailors are supposed to be kept, but he had never fancied it. Messy, it sounded, as though things would have been nibbled at, and, of all things, Arriman hated a *mess*.

Then he had an idea and smiled. "Hand me my wand, Leadbetter," he said, and shut his eyes. The next second a large gray skeleton stuck together with bits of wire swirled through the air and landed at the sea witch's feet.

"I wanted a *fresh* one," complained Ms. Wrack. "One with some meat on him. It's for bait."

"If witch number one is not satisfied," snapped Arriman, fire shooting from his nostrils, "she may withdraw from the contest."

"Oh, all right," said Mabel sulkily. "But he's a very funny shape."

This was certainly true. The skeleton had, in fact, belonged to the biology lab of a large comprehensive school in the Midlands, and the poor gentleman hadn't exactly been a sailor but an undertaker who liked messing about in boats and had fallen, in the year 1892, into the Shropshire Union Canal. Owing to the carelessness of the children, and the fact that the biology master was the kind who couldn't keep order, the skeleton had got badly jumbled. The skull was back to front, three finger bones were missing, and for some reason he seemed to have had three thighs.

"Announce the trick you will perform," Mr. Leadbetter shouted through his megaphone.

Mabel Wrack turned to face the judges. She had taken Doris out of her bucket and thrown the familiar's tentacles carelessly round her shoulders like a mink stole, while she held the animal's round body under her arm, squeezing it for power and darkness like someone playing the bagpipes.

Then she spoke.

"I SHALL CALL FORTH THE KRAKEN FROM THE DEEP," she said.

There was a stunned silence. The Kraken! That dread and dangerous monster that has lain since the dawn of time beneath the surface of the sea, dragging ships to their doom, creating by its lightest movement, tidal waves that could drown cities!

"Oh, Terence," whispered Belladonna, "I'm scared, aren't you? Fancy Mabel Wrack being able to do *that*!"

And indeed all the onlookers were a little bit ashamed. They had never taken the fishy witch too seriously and now . . .

Even Arriman the Awful was impressed. "Instruct witch number one to proceed," he said.

Mabel Wrack stepped forward to the edge of the ocean. The sea witch was no slouch, and she had prepared her act with care. She would begin by peppering the sea with golden rings to fetch up the underwater spirits who were known to be extremely fond of jewelry and would then come and help her when she called them to her aid. As for the drowned sailor, he was meant to lure the Kraken from his lair and so make it easier for the spirits to find him.

She put Doris back in her bucket and threw the rings one by one into the foam. Then she raised her arms, and the skeleton of the undertaker who had liked messing about in boats rose slowly up in the air, turned a somersault, and tumbled into the waves.

"Levitation," said Arriman. "Quite neat. Give her a mark for that, don't you think?" The thought of seeing a Kraken had quite cheered him up.

Next, Mabel picked up the gong and thumped it with a resounding wallop, which sent the seabirds flying up in terror. Then:

> *"Mighty Spirits of the Deep*
> *Pray you waken from your sleep.*
> *Come as fast as you are able*
> *Come and help your sister, Mabel,"*

chanted Ms. Wrack. She had decided to go into poetry for the contest. This may have been a mistake. Some witches have a feeling for poetry, some haven't. Ms. Wrack hadn't.

> *"From thunderous reef and mighty grot*
> *The dreaded Kraken must be got. . . ."*

"What's a grot?" whispered Mother Bloodwort pettishly from behind the gorse bushes.

"It's short for grotto, I think," Belladonna whispered back. "Sort of a cave." Though she knew that she had no chance of winning now—who could do any-thing more terrible than call up a Kraken—she was looking at Ms. Wrack with shining eyes. There just wasn't a mean streak anywhere in Belladonna.

The pause which followed was an anxious one. Even Arriman wondered if he had been hasty. Would there be flooding? Whirlpools? Cannibalism? There are too many stories of witches summoning up evil forces which they cannot then control.

The pause lengthened. The ghoul, unable to take the strain, dropped off to sleep, and still the wind soughed, and the gray sea foamed and boiled against the rocks.

But now there was a change. The sky seemed to darken. The white crests of the waves died away to leave a creeping, wrinkled skin of water. The wind dropped. The sea birds fell silent.

What came next was a strange heaping up of the water into a mound that grew and grew and became a huge tower topped with foam. And now the tower reared upward, bent, and turned to race—a great tun-nel of boiling, churning water—toward the shore.

The witches huddled together. Terence's hand crept into Belladonna's, and at the judges' table, Arriman reached for the genie's bottle and screwed on the top.

Just in time. The towering wave had landed with a thunderous crash upon the sand. And when the foam and turmoil had died down, the onlookers blinked.

Ms. Wrack had called on the spirits of the deep to help her find the Kraken, and it was perhaps natural that these should be mermaids. But the four ladies who now sat on the beach were fleshy and no longer young, and they seemed to be rather pointlessly clutching a large black handbag, each of them holding on to it with a pudgy arm. The rings which Ms. Wrack had sent them glistened on their fingers, and their lower halves were sensibly covered in tail cozies of knitted bladder wrack, but all of them were topless, and Arriman had already flinched and closed his eyes.

Ms. Wrack stepped closer—and her mouth opened in horror.

"Septic suckerfish!" she swore under her breath.

And indeed it was the most appalling luck! Of all the mermaids in the ocean, she had managed to call up her mother's four unmarried sisters: Aunt Edna, Aunt Gwendolyn, Aunt Phoebe, and Aunt Jane!

For a moment, Mabel panicked. There is probably nothing less black or magical in the whole world than a person's aunt. Then she remembered that the top half of her face was covered by a mask. With luck, she would not be recognized. There had been a bit of a split in the family when her mother had opted for legs. So, disguising her voice as well as she could, she began:

> *"Summoned here, I bid thee hearken,*
> *You have been to fetch the Kraken*
> *Search the corners of the ocean—"*

She broke off, trying to find a rhyme for "ocean," and also wondering a bit whether an ocean really *had* corners. But she needn't have bothered because all four of her aunts were talking at once, taking no notice of each other or of her.

"My dear, we're so glad you called! We've been worried *sick*!"

"Not knowing what to do for the best, you see."

"When that oil rig went through his mother's head—"

"Skull shattered; not a hope, poor soul—"

"It's *meant*, I said to Edna, didn't I, dear?"

"You did, Phoebe. It's *meant*, you said."

"*Someone* knows what's right."

The aunt who had just spoken broke off, edged closer, peered at Mabel Wrack. "Funny, I'd swear I'd seen you before. Those nostrils . . . that mouth . . ."

Still clutching their handbag, the mermaids waddled toward her on their tails.

"It can't be, of course. But isn't she the *spit* of poor Agatha!"

"The spit!" echoed Aunt Jane.

Mabel Wrack retreated backward, but it was too late.

"It *must* be Agatha's little girl. The one she had with the fishmonger after the operation. It *is* her, I'm sure. Mabel, wasn't she called?"

"Mabel! Dear little Mabel!"

Terribly exicited, the aunts dropped their handbag at last and surrounded their niece with a great flopping of tails and waving of pink, plump arms.

"Stop it!" hissed Mabel furiously. "This is a competition. Keep *away*! And speak in verse, you're disgracing me."

There was a moment of outraged silence while Mabel continued to glare angrily at her relations. It was a silly thing for her to do. Mermaids are famous for being touchy, and so, of course, are maiden aunts.

"Oh, very well," said Aunt Edna haughtily. "We know when we aren't wanted, don't we?"

"It was you that called *us*, you know."

"Such airs—just because her father had legs and a shop."

As they spoke, the mermaids began to waddle huffily away, speaking over their shoulders as they went.

"We were going to stay and give you a few hints, but we won't bother now."

"Don't blame *us* if you don't know how much sieved sea quirt to give."

"Speak in verse, indeed!"

And with a last, offended sniff, the four mermaids dived back into the water and were gone.

"Stop!" shouted the desperate Ms. Wrack. "Come back! You've left your handbag!"

It was a dreadful moment. The mermaids had gone, the mighty Kraken still slumbered beneath the deep, and on the face of Arriman the Awful there was a look that froze the marrow in one's bones.

And now this handbag . . .

Only, was it a handbag? For even as they watched, the object on the sand seemed to give a kind of judder. Next it puffed itself out into a round, smoothed dome like the top of a tadpole or of a small and very squidgy flying saucer. In the middle of this dome, two slits now appeared and a pair of shining, tear-filled, sky-blue eyes stared upward at Ms. Wrack.

"Oh, my gawd," said Lester, with whom the penny had already dropped.

The thing now went into a kind of private struggle and from its round, dark blancmange of a body there appeared, one by one, eight wavery, wobbly legs, each ending in a blob-shaped foot. Peering closer, the onlookers could see, at the rim of the saucer, a round hole from whose reddened edges the little finger bone of the undertaker sadly hung. Aunt Jane had given it to him to help him with his teething.

Even with the evidence there before their eyes, no one could quite believe it. They watched in silence as the "handbag" raised itself once more, tottered a few pathetic steps, and fell in a despairing, quivering heap before Ms. Wrack.

"Mummy?" it said in a piteous voice. "Mummy?"

The sea witch stepped back in disgust; Terence clung tightly to Belladonna to stop her running forward; the ghoul woke suddenly and said: "Spittle!"; and Arriman the Awful rose from his seat.

"What in the name of devilry and darkness is that THING?" he thundered.

He knew, of course. You could say a lot about Arriman, but not that he was thick.

"That, sir," said the ogre, "is a Kraken. A baby Kraken. A very young baby Kraken indeed."

Hearing voices, feeling himself unwanted by the very witch who had called him from the sea, the Kraken, his eyes, his whole body streaming with tears, now began to totter wetly to the table where the judges sat. Three times he fell, his legs hopelessly knotted, and three times he rose again, leaving each time a glistening pool of water, until he reached the chair of Arriman the Awful, Wizard of the North.

"Daddy?" said the Kraken, rolling his anguished eyes upward. And again: "Daddy?"

Everybody waited.

Arriman looked downward and shuddered. "Take it away, Lester. Remove it. Throw it back into the sea."

The ogre did not move.

"You heard me, Lester. It is dribbling on my feet."

"Sir," said the ogre. "That Kraken is an orphan. Its mother's had an oil rig through her head. It'll be two thousand years before that Kraken is old enough to swallow as much as a canoe. If you throw it back now, it'll die."

"So?" said Arriman nastily.

Over by the gorse bushes, Belladonna closed her eyes and prayed. Mr. Chatterjee tried to swoosh out of his bottle, hit his head on the screwed-on top, and fell back, his turban over his dark, kind face.

"Daddy?" said the Kraken, his voice only a whisper now—and raised from the top of his body, a tiny, trembling, and hopeless-looking tail.

"Oh, a plague on the lot of you," cursed Arriman, and scooping up the Kraken, which immediately began to squeak and giggle because it was extremely ticklish, the furious magician left the judges' table and strode away toward the hall.

CHAPTER 9

*M*ABEL'S MARKS WERE announced that night. She had scored four out of a possible ten—a low mark and one that would have been lower if Arriman had had his way. But as kind Mr. Chatterjee pointed out, she had called up the Kraken from the deep and it wasn't her fault that the thing had turned out the way it had.

The low score pleased all the other witches, and Ethel Feedbag, whose turn came on the following day, was heard lurching and roistering round the campfire until long after midnight, hiccuping over her parsnip wine, and falling asleep with her head on her pig and her Wellies dangerously close to the embers. Belladonna, of course, couldn't help feeling a bit sorry for Mabel, who had retired huffily into her sleeping bag with wet towels around her legs, but Terence didn't pretend to be anything but pleased.

"You'll see, Belladonna, you'll win; you're bound to!"

He had brought Rover down earlier, and just by touching the slender, peaceful body of her familiar, Belladonna had been able to turn the passionflowers into bloodshot eyeballs and the golden pears into thumbscrews. She'd left the baby rabbits because, as she said to Terence, it was knowing that she *could* turn them into decayed appendixes that was important.

"How is . . . you know . . . He?" she asked now.

Terence said that Arriman was a little bit upset. He could have said more, but he knew that Belladonna was in love and that nothing hurts people more than to think that someone they love is not altogether perfect. In fact, Arriman had been yelling like nobody's business on account of the Kraken. Absolutely nothing could persuade the Kraken that Arriman was not his father, and the magician had had to change his shoes three times between tea and supper because the thing insisted on sitting on his feet. Krakens make their own wetness from the inside and can breathe in air as well as in water so there was nothing to stop the dreaded denizen of the deep from trying to climb onto Arriman's lap or shedding tears all over his trousers, and the great man was taking it very badly.

"Oh, why didn't the new wizard cometh!" he raged at dinner. "I'd have been spared all this. Lester, take it away!"

"It's you he wants, sir," said the ogre reproachfully. But he scooped the Kraken up and put him in a soup tureen, for what with Sir Simon wailing in the wainscot, Mr. Chatterjee sneezing in his bottle, and the ghoul dribbling raw liver from his mouth, he did feel that perhaps his master had had enough.

The following morning they were up early to see what witch number two was going to do.

Ethel had chosen to perform her trick in a grassy and very beautiful hollow in which, beside a bubbling brook, there grew an oak, an ash, and a thorn.

These three trees have, since the beginning of time, been special trees. Even separately they are special but when they grow together . . . well, anything can happen in a place like that.

"Witch number two—step forward!" shouted Mr. Leadbetter, and Ethel, still wearing beneath her gown the three moldering jerseys she'd slept in, lurched out from behind a rock, pushing a wheelbarrow and calling to her huge and mucky pig.

"Hand in your list!" Mr. Leadbetter ordered, and Ethel walked over to the judges' table, which Lester had set out on a level patch of grass, and put down a crumpled piece of paper in front of Arriman.

The magician read it and passed a weary hand across his forehead. Witch number two wanted: *A man, a woman, and a child.*

"More fuss," he murmured. And then: "Fetch the telephone directory."

So Terence ran up to the hall and came back with the *Todcaster and District Directory,* and Arriman closed his eyes, flicked the pages, and stubbed his finger down on what turned out to be the Bs.

It is not difficult to work a telephone directory. Any wizard worth his salt can do it. You just press your finger down hard on a telephone number, say the right spells, and immediately you can see in your mind's eye the family that lives at that address. After that, summoning them by levitation is just child's play. So now Arriman ignored a Colonel Bellingbotter sitting pinkly in his bath at Todcaster 5930, passed over the Bender sisters doing keep-fit exercise at 2378, and found in the Bicknell family, at Todcaster 9549, exactly what he was looking for.

Mr. and Mrs. Bicknell and their daughter, Linda, were sitting at breakfast in their small semi at 187 Acacia Avenue. Mrs. Bicknell was still in her hair net and curlers; Linda was dressed for school. Linda was fat and her mother was thin; Linda was eight years old and her mother was thirty-five, but what they both liked best was being nasty to Linda's father, Mr. Bicknell, and they were doing it now.

"Why did you put on that stupid shirt?" said Mrs. Bicknell. "It makes you look like an ostrich with the croup."

"Your hair's getting awfully thin on top, Daddy! You'll be bald soon. Won't you look silly when you're bald," said Linda.

"Mrs. Pearce across the road is getting a new washing machine. I suppose you know I've had *my* washing machine for three years?"

"Davina's daddy's buying her a doll that can clean its own teeth. Why don't *you* buy me a doll like that?"

Mr. Bicknell, a small, rather stooped man with a thin, tired face and a lined forehead, just went on quietly eating his cornflakes. He worked hard all day in his grocer's shop, helping the people he served to make their money go further, and when he came home at night he went on helping. He helped his wife with the washing up and fixed shelves and dug the garden, but whatever he did, it made no difference. His wife and his daughter just nagged and nagged and nagged.

"You didn't clean the budgerigar's cage out properly," said Mrs. Bicknell, piling her toast with marmalade. "There's birdseed stuck to the corner."

"Davina says being a grocer is *silly*. Only *silly* people are grocers, Davina says."

"And I wish that just for once you'd—"

But at this point the windows began to rattle violently. Then they burst open and the room was filled with a whirling, roaring wind which lifted Mr. and Mrs. Bicknell and their daughter, Linda, and sent them up and out of the house . . . up and away . . . to land, in what seemed to be just a moment in time, at Ethel Feedbag's feet.

The country witch peered down at them and nodded. Then she stuck her boot under the shrieking, twitching Mrs. Bicknell and the howling, kicking Linda and turned them over on their backs. There was no need to turn over Mr. Bicknell who already lay quietly, looking upward at the sky.

"Announce your trick!" commanded Mr. Leadbetter through his megaphone.

Ethel took the straw from her mouth, burped, and said: "I BE GOIN' TO SHUT THE WOMAN IN THE ASH TREE AN' THE MAN IN THE OAK TREE AN' THAT BAWLIN' BRAT IN THE THORN TREE."

A whisper passed through the audience and they looked at witch number two with a new respect. Imprisonment of human beings in trees is very old magic and it is as black as night. The druids did it, and the witches of ancient Greece and Rome. Even now there are gaunt willows and shuddering alders from whose insides their own spirits have fled, to be replaced by some boastful traveler or careless shepherd who has lain there trapped in slumber for a thousand years.

Only Belladonna, hiding with the other witches, was unhappy. "Those *poor* trees!" she murmured.

And indeed the trees were worth worrying about. The oak was one of those trees that are a whole world of their own: its great scarred trunk was full of clefts and hollows in which squirrels lived, and mice and little scurrying beetles. It stood rooted in a pool of soft green moss; delicate acorn cups clung to its mazed branches, and its crown was a mass of autumn gold.

The ash was as tall, but slender, the smooth gray bark seemingly like silver against the pale blue sky, the key-shaped seeds hanging in bunches from its upward-sweeping boughs. A younger tree than the oak, but proud and regal as a queen.

And lastly, the hawthorn, a most powerful and knowing tree with its writhing trunk, its bloodred berries clustered around the fierce black barbs.

Ethel Feedbag, meanwhile, had fetched a sack from her wheelbarrow and humped it to where the Bicknells lay. It was labeled MANGEL WURZEL MEAL, but it was better not to ask what was really in the powder she now sprinkled over the bawling, slug-faced Linda, her twitching mother, and the tired body of the grocer. Whatever it was, within seconds all three of them lay unconscious on the grass.

Grinning happily, Ethel now pulled up her gown, fumbled under her skirt, and from the elastic of her brown woolen knickers, drew a long black-hilted witches' knife. And as she did so, Arriman gasped and turned a chalky white. He had seen, clear as daylight, the dreaded Wellies beneath the gown.

For a moment, it looked as though the great magician would cut and run, but the ogre and the secretary had already closed ranks behind him, and with a groan he sank back in his seat.

Ethel, meanwhile, was smearing the bark of the thorn tree with a slimy blood-colored paste. Then she picked up her knife and made a single, long slit in its side.

"Oh, Terence, I can't *bear* it!" whispered Belladonna.

"I don't suppose it feels any pain, Belladonna. I expect that's what the ointment was for. To stop it hurting."

They watched breathlessly as the slit, of its own accord, grew wider . . . wider . . . and became, at last, a gaping hole that led to the tree's very heart.

"Not bad," said Arriman, struggling to be fair. "Though I prefer lightning myself. Neater."

Ethel grunted, whacked her pig, and came back to stand with her knife poised over Linda.

"Is she going to kill her?" asked Terence hopefully.

But Ethel was crouching over Linda, murmuring a

spell in a language so ancient and peculiar that none of them could make out a word. Over and over again she chanted, and then slowly the fat, nasty little schoolgirl rose from the grass, stuck her hands in front of her, and began to sleepwalk, like a bewitched suet pudding, toward the tree.

"In!" ordered Ethel, putting a boot in Linda's bottom.

And, lo and behold, Linda wobbled forward into the thorn tree and the sides of the tree came together closer . . . closer . . . and the slit vanished and she was gone.

Next, Ethel went over to the ash. Again she rubbed the tree with ointment, again she made a slit in its side, and again the slit widened to show the dark center of the tree. And now it was Mrs. Bicknell who rose and walked in a trance into the tree and the tree closed around her, and she was gone.

Ethel was just going to start the oak when there was an extremely angry *rustling* noise which began at the hawthorn tree and moved over to where Ethel stood. A second, even angrier rustle, followed. What these were, were the spirits of the thorn and of the ash, and they were in a very nasty temper indeed.

"It is not at *all* convenient for me to be out this morning," said the spirit of the ash.

"You might have *asked*," said the spirit of the thorn.

One cannot actually see tree spirits—they are simply a rustle—but one knows that if one could, they would be green, female, and easily upset.

"Didn't ask you to shift," said Ethel. "Plenty of room for everybody."

"Stay in with that repulsive child!" said the spirit of the thorn. "You must be joking! I'm going home to Mother." And she rustled off in the direction of an old hawthorn standing on the hill, followed by the spirit of the ash, still yammering with indignation.

Ethel shrugged. It took more than a couple of rustles to upset a Feedbag. She had made a slit in the oak tree now and stood back as it opened, groaning and creaking and sending the squirrels and dormice scampering away in terror.

Then Ethel went to fetch Mr. Bicknell and he, too, got up and walked into the tree, and the tree closed over him, and he was gone.

The judges, going over to have a closer look, were pleased. True, the thorn tree bulged at the bottom because of the fatness of Linda's thighs, and its bark had come out in bumpy knots like boils. The golden leaves of the ash, too, were shriveling fast. Still, no passerby could possibly have guessed that three frantic, tortured human beings were imprisoned in this peaceful dell.

But of course there was no question of giving out marks just yet. A true witch must be able to loosen an enchantment as well as weave it.

"Undo the spell!" ordered Arriman.

Ethel had slumped down beside her pig. Now she got up and waddled over to the thorn. Again she made a slit in the tree, again the slit widened—and out on the grass like a crumpled maggot rolled Linda Bicknell.

Next, Ethel slit open the ash, and the lovely tree seemed to sigh with relief as Mrs. Bicknell, sticky with sap and minus three of her curlers, fell out onto the turf.

Smirking now, Ethel went over to the oak. Again she slit it, again she stood back and waited.

Nothing happened.

"Out!" ordered Ethel, jerking her head.

Still nothing.

Beneath the mask, Ethel's round face flushed with temper.

"Out!" she said, stamping her foot.

Silence. Then, from the depths of the great tree, a quiet voice said: *"No!"*

Ethel's face darkened to beetroot. "It's over," she hissed. "You come on out!"

But inside the oak tree, the tired grocer did not stir. What did come out of the tree was its spirit. Like the spirits of the ash and of the thorn, the spirit of the oak was simply a rustle but an older and a wiser one.

"Leave him be," it said to Ethel Feedbag. "He wants to stay. He likes it in there. Says he'll come out when his wife's ninety and in a wheelchair and can't nag, and his daughter's left home for good."

"Stay in t' tree?" roared Ethel, angry as a bull.

"That's right," rustled the spirit. "Says he's never been so happy in his life. He's no bother to me; he just wants to sleep most of the time. His wife used to snore and kick him around the bed, you know how some women do. I don't mind him, he's company— and you can see *he* doesn't mind."

This was true. Unlike the thorn which had come out in boils, or the ash whose leaves had shriveled, the great oak tree stood calm and undisturbed by the grocer in his depths.

"Just do us up again, dear," ordered the spirit. "It's getting drafty. He'll be all right in there for fifty years or so; I'll see he doesn't go moldy. Then someone can let him out and the poor bloke can lead a decent life."

So Ethel closed the tree up again. What else could she do? But when Linda and her mother had been sent back to Acacia Avenue and Ethel's marks came through, they were low; four out of ten, the same as Mabel's. What else could one expect? There is nothing black about shutting someone into a tree who simply loves it there.

But if Ethel was furious, Arriman was as happy as a lark. Whatever else happened, he wouldn't have to marry the witch with the Wellies. All through supper he laughed and joked—until he went upstairs, heard the steady drip-drip of water, and found that the Kraken had climbed onto his bed.

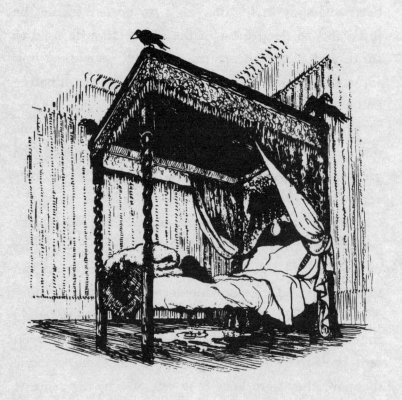

CHAPTER 10

NO ONE EVER FORGOT what happened when witch number three did her trick. It was really very horrible in a way that no one could have imagined, and even Arriman, used as he was to terror and disaster, could never think of it, in years to come, without feeling quite giddy and faint.

Witch number three was Nancy Shouter, and when she announced her trick there was a great deal of interest.

"I AM GOING," she said, "TO MAKE A BOTTOMLESS HOLE."

To make a bottomless hole is not easy. A bottomless hole is not a hole that comes out in Australia; a hole that comes out in Australia is a hole that comes out in Australia—it is not bottomless. No, bottomless is something very different. Bottomlessness is a mysterious nothingness that goes on forever; it is an interminable blackness; it is no echo, no plop when something drops into it, no glimmer of water in its depths. Not only that, a bottomless hole has a demonic and unusual power—anyone coming too close has an almost uncontrollable longing to throw himself into it.

Everyone, therefore, was pleased, and Mr. Chatterjee, becoming muddled in his excitement, said, "Oh, that is good! A bottom with no hole!"

So Nancy got to work. She had chosen the east lawn, quite close to the house, to do her trick, and she went about it in a businesslike manner, stubbing out her cigarette, putting her chicken down on the bonnet of the caterpillar tractor that Mr. Leadbetter had hired for her, and setting the motor in motion so that the heavy rotary blades could dig into the soil.

It was a mild and pleasant day. The other witches were clustered in the little summer house, where they could see without being seen by Arriman. Even Madame Olympia had turned out with her aardvark. At the judges' table, which Lester had raised on wooden blocks so that they could see the digging better, Arriman tried to forget the awful night he'd spent with the Kraken, and his anxiety about the Wizard Watcher (who was sending brave but homesick postcards from places like Brighton and Southend-on-Sea), and prepared to give witch number three a chance.

Nancy certainly seemed to know her job. True, her chicken was against her. All along, the Shouter chickens had been rather a washout as familiars. They never crowed thrice or flapped threateningly or erected their wattles, and altogether they looked more like old-age pensioners evicted from a battery than the kind of bird one finds in fairy stories or in fights.

All the same, Nancy was doing all right. From working with the railway, both the Shouter twins were good with mechanical things, and after about an hour Nancy drove the tractor away to the other side of the lawn and the real task began.

Because, of course, at this stage the thing was simply a hole. Nancy had dug up some old drainpipes, part of a tin bath, an old ham bone of the Wizard Watcher's, and masses and masses of shale and sludge. She had made a deep hole, a good hole, the kind of hole little boys stand and gape at on the way to school, but though its bottom was a long way down, it was still *there.*

But now the magic began. First Nancy circled the hole with her wand, scratching a witches' pentacle deep into the surrounding soil. Five times she walked widdershins round the hole and five times she walked *not* widdershins, keeping always to the far side of the magic symbol. Then she put down her wand, picked up her chicken, and, raising it aloft, turned to the north.

"Spirits of the earth, I bid thee SUCK THE BOTTOM FROM THIS HOLE!" she intoned.

Then, still holding her chicken, she turned to the west: "Spirits of fire, I bid thee BURN THE BOTTOM FROM THIS HOLE!" cried Nancy Shouter.

Then she turned to the east and bade the spirits of the air BLOW THE BOTTOM FROM THE HOLE. But now, the chicken had had enough. It fluttered, squawking, from her arms, and it was chickenless that Nancy turned to the south and commanded the spirits of the water to DROWN THE BOTTOM OF THE HOLE.

After which she said the Lord's Prayer backward—and the spell was complete.

It is always hard, the bit between the end of a piece of magic and the time when it is supposed to work. No one is good at waiting, and witches least of all. Nancy had begun most irritably to tap her toes when the scream began.

It was a scream such as no one could have imagined. A scream as if a million giants were being disembow-eled with red-hot pincers—a scream that grew louder and more unendurable each second, till everyone present thought that their skulls must shatter with the pain of it.

And how could it be otherwise? For this was the

scream of a hole losing the only thing it has—its bottom.

When the noise had died away at last and the pain in their ears had gone, the judges walked over to where Nancy stood. Taking care not to go too close because of the fearsome power a bottomless hole has to draw things into it, they examined, discussed, and considered.

And they were pleased. Arriman was nodding, Mr. Chatterjee, in his bright turban, was bobbing up and down, and the white exhausted face of the old ghoul had cracked into something almost like a smile.

For while it is true that there is not much you can actually *do* with a bottomless hole, at least it cannot possibly turn out to be someone's aunt like the mermaids, nor can it make anybody happy as Mr. Bicknell had been made happy by being shut into a tree. As they returned to the table, it was clear that the judges were going to give Nancy a much higher mark than they had awarded to Ethel Feedbag or Mabel Wrack.

But before they could make an announcement there was a scuffle from the summer house; Belladonna cried: "Oh, please, don't!"—and then Nora Shouter, shaking herself loose, catapulted onto the east lawn, brandishing her chicken as she came.

"You're a cheat!" she screamed, charging up to her twin. "You're a liar and a twister and a cheat! That's *my* chicken you've got there! You've done your trick with *my* chicken so it doesn't count."

"I have *not* done my trick with your chicken! I have done my trick with *my* chicken!"

"You haven't!"

"You have!"

Face-to-face on the east lawn, the Shouter sisters' fury and loathing reached new heights.

"And anyway," yelled Nora, "I don't believe your hole is bottomless. It's just a hole!"

"My hole is *so* bottomless!"

"No, it isn't!"

"Yes, it is!"

Arriman had risen from his seat, his devilish eyebrows meeting in an angry frown, and in the summer house, Belladonna covered her face. But nothing could stop the Shouters now. Both had put down their chickens and stood facing each other with murder in their eyes.

"If you say my hole isn't bottomless once more, I'll finish you, you worm-eaten stick," screamed Nancy, forgetting the contest, forgetting everything.

"It isn't bottomless! It isn't bottomless! It isn't bottomless!" screamed Nora, quite eaten up with jealousy and temper.

What happened next, happened with terrifying speed.

Nancy stepped forward and pushed her sister hard, sending her reeling, to fall backward with her legs in the air. Then, as Nora tried to rise, Nancy pushed her again and she fell, this time inside the magic pentacle.

Even then, Nancy might have saved her twin. But she stood there, unmoving, her face suffused with an evil, gloating triumph as Nora half rose, swayed—and tottered, *of her own accord,* toward the round, black maw. . . . Right at the edge, she managed to pause, and tried desperately to take a step backward. Too late! There was a hideous, roaring, sucking noise, Nora's arm went up. . . . And then the hole took her and she was gone.

The campsite, that night, was silent as the grave. Arriman, white with shock, had disqualified witch number three and ordered the east lawn to be cleared. Nancy, though, had hardly seemed to hear what he said, but just stood there, blindly gazing at the spot where her sister had last stood, and in the end it was Belladonna who led her away and put her to bed in the tent she had shared with Nora.

"Doesn't matter which of our chickens is which now, does it?" was all Nancy said as Belladonna settled the sad brown birds into their coops.

And Belladonna, who knew perfectly well which chicken was which, and always had, agreed that it didn't matter now. It didn't matter at all.

The horribleness of what had happened kept everyone in a state of shock throughout the following day, which was the one on which Nora should have done her act. Mr. Chatterjee stayed curled in his bottle like a baby that doesn't want to be born, Arriman didn't even notice when the Kraken dribbled into his best elastic-sided boots, and at the campsite the witches stopped bickering for once, shamed by the tragedy that had overtaken them.

But the strangest thing of all was what had happened to Nancy.

Nancy had turned overnight from a loudmouthed, bossy, chain-smoking witch into a timid, shrunken person who just lay on her camp bed in her vest and knickers refusing to wash or dress or eat, and telling anyone who came near that it didn't matter which chicken was which.

"She's going off her nut, you mark my words," said Mother Bloodwort. "I've seen it before. She's flipped."

Terence couldn't understand it. "She hated Nora so *much*, didn't she, Belladonna? So why is she so upset?"

Belladonna crinkled her forehead, trying to work it out.

"I suppose . . . hating Nora was sort of a *part* of

133

Nancy. I mean, it was what being Nancy was *about.* And now Nora's gone, she isn't anybody. Just a wraith."

But however worried they were about Nancy, the contest had to go on. So later that afternoon, Terence and Belladonna set off for the woods behind the campsite and practiced with Rover, turning the golden bracken fronds into leprous fingers and conjuring little spitting dragons from a bramble bush. They had discovered that Rover's power was so strong that it could work from *inside* the matchbox even when Terence held it closed, and this was a great help because with the box open, Rover had wandered about rather a lot.

"Funny, I thought I heard someone moving over there, behind those elms," said Belladonna, as they sat resting in a grassy clearing, letting Rover crawl confidingly across their hands.

They peered through the trees, but there was no one there. Yet both of them had had an eerie feeling of being watched, and by someone far more sinister than lumbering Ethel or fishy Mabel Wrack.

"Perhaps we'd better put him away," said Terence, scooping Rover back into his box. They had kept his incredible power secret from the other witches and they meant to go on doing so.

And if they could not see the cunning enchantress

loping away from the clearing, who could blame them? She had taken on a form much used by witches: that of a fleet and silent hare. But no real hare ever had in its eyes the look that was in this one's: evil and calculating and unutterably cruel.

CHAPTER 11

THE FOLLOWING DAY it was Mother Bloodwort's turn. She had spent the whole of the evening
before in a last desperate attempt at the turning-
herself-young-again spell, rushing from her tent to
the toilet block and back again with little jars of
crushed gall bladder from the inside of murderers,
powdered mandrake picked under a dying moon, and
a whole lot of other noxious things which she rubbed
into herself, croaking weird rhymes as she did so.

But it hadn't helped. As she was announced by Mr.
Leadbetter and tottered out into the Italian garden,
she was unmistakably Mother Bloodwort, warts, whiskers, cloud of flies, and all.

Arriman of course, recognized her at once. But to
the surprise of Mr. Leadbetter and the ogre, he did
not try to escape. The reason for this was simple. He

had decided that if the witch with the whiskers won the contest, he, Arriman the Awful, would kill himself. He would do this in some very dramatic way, perhaps by plunging over the cliff into the boiling waters of the Devil's Cauldron, or by shooting himself with a silver dueling pistol, or by falling onto one of the swords that Lester was always swallowing, but he would do it.

So he was quite calm as witch number five hobbled toward him and handed in her list, and he stayed calm until he'd read it.

It was Mother Bloodwort who wanted the seven princesses. She was going to do an old-fashioned trick, but a very famous one: the one in which seven beautiful maidens of the blood royal turn into seven black swans, doomed to wing their way across the waters of the world through all eternity.

There is probably nothing sadder or more romantic in all magic than this spell. One minute you have these lively, bright-eyed girls with all life before them, and often a prince or two in the offing—and then there comes this ghastly moment when their golden hair turns into black down, their rosebud mouths become beaks, their pretty feet in silver slippers change into webbed toes . . . until at last the great black tragic birds fly away into the sunset never to return.

As a setting for this trick, Mother Bloodwort had chosen the Italian garden, which lay beside the lake.

Arriman hadn't got round to much blighting and smiting there, and it was a beautiful spot with urns, statues, and wide gravel paths which swept down to the shimmering water.

But now the great magician had read her list. "Seven princesses!" he roared. "Seven! You must be mad!"

Mother Bloodwort, however, was not to be put off.

"Aye. Seven. Proper ones. Royal."

"I can't just whirl princesses through the air like commoners, you know," said Arriman. "The thing has to be done properly. Decent transport and all that. And they're not in the telephone directory."

But Mother Bloodwort, obstinate old witch that she was, just stood there, waiting.

Arriman sighed. "Tell everyone to go away for an hour, Leadbetter," he said. "I'll have to go to my laboratory for this. And send me that nephew of yours. He's a useful lad, and I could do with an extra pair of hands."

So Mr. Leadbetter took the witches back to the camp, and Terence, beaming with pride, followed Arriman and the ogre into the laboratory with its bubbling crucibles and fiendish flasks.

"Actually there is a *sort* of telephone directory for princesses," said the magician. "It's called the *Almanach de Gotha.* Run and get it from the library, boy. It's a big, gold-bound book on the second shelf as you go in."

Terence was back in no time, his eyes shining with excitement.

"Hm," said Arriman. "Let's see. There's a Spanish family descended from Carlos the Cruel, I believe. Yes . . . good, there seems to be a daughter. And we ought to find something in Austria. What about the Habsburgs—they're certainly royal enough."

"Can't we have a *British* princess?" said Lester.

Arriman shook his head. "Not wise, I think." He continued to flick the pages. "We shall have to scrape the barrel a bit. Still, let's get to work."

For nearly an hour, Arriman magicked: murmuring spells, twirling his wand, going backward and forward between his potions and his vellum-bound books. Once he said: "Strange, I feel an unusual force in this room. Things are coming through much faster than usual." But though Terence exchanged a look with Lester, he said nothing. Rover was in his pocket, but if Belladonna was to win the contest, the worm's special power *had* to be kept a secret.

"Right," said the magician. "You can fetch them all back now. The last one's just come through."

Because, sure enough, there, rather beautifully arranged round the rim of a fountain, were seven princesses. Arriman had kept his word and all of them were of the blood royal, but that was as far as he'd been able to go. It was no use pretending that they were a matching set of lovely girls. The Princess Olga Zerchinsky, for example, a niece of one of the last grand dukes of Russia, was ninety-two and crippled with rheumatism so that Arriman had had to conjure her up in a wheelchair. On the other hand, an African princess, descended from King Solomon himself, was lying asleep in her cradle. The Spanish princess, though beautifully dressed in couture, unfortunately had a wooden leg, and the Indian princess was almost invisible in a cloud of exhaust from her motorcycle. There was another young princess from America wearing Levi's and a T-shirt emblazoned with *I AM BATMAN'S FRIEND* (her ancestors had left France when Louis Philippe lost his throne), and there was a middle-aged Austrian one whose nose came down over her chin because she was a Habsburg and they have been famous through history for being the ugliest rulers in the world. And there was an Eastern princess in silken trousers who had Mr. Chatterjee swooshing out of his bottle with excitement.

Mother Bloodwort, meanwhile, had announced her trick. "I AM GOING TO TURN SEVEN PRINCESSES OF THE BLOOD ROYAL INTO SEVEN BLACK SWANS," she said. Then, feeling perhaps that something was missing, she added: "TEE HEE," which was the nearest she could get to evil, cackling laughter.

She then vanished behind a statue of the god, Pan, and returned with a broomstick. It was the crummiest, most moth-eaten broomstick anyone had ever seen— Mother Bloodwort had made it herself from brush- wood she had found at the back of the camping site—but everyone was pleased because it meant she was going to do hobbyhorse magic. This is the kind where you ride round and round your victims going faster and ever faster, dizzying them with your speed and

your spells, until the transformation is complete. It is old-fashioned magic, but it can be very powerful.

So now Mother Bloodwort went over to the foun- tain, blew a hole in her cloud of flies, and stood peer- ing at the princesses. Then she laid her wrinkled hand on the Spanish one in her turquoise gown.

"You!" she said, pulling her forward on to the gravel path.

Arriman had hypnotized the princesses as they came so that Princess Juanita followed the old crone obedi- ently, her wooden leg clacking a little as she walked.

Mother Bloodwort now mounted her broomstick, groaning as she heaved her stiff old legs over the handle, which she had greased with the melted body fat of maddened skunks, and began to ride around and around the royal Spanish lady.

"Hattock away, ye magic broom
Send this princess to her doom!"

shrieked Mother Bloodwort.

Faster she rode, and faster, sending her hood tumbling back and her white hair streaming, while her cloud of flies clung desperately to her flushed face and heaving chest.

So crazy did she look, so exhausted and old, that no one really expected the magic to work. But they were wrong. Strange and terrible things were happening to the Princess Juanita.

Her hair had wavered . . . vanished. . . . Her head was shimmering . . . and now it was covered in feathers, and her full, pouting mouth was changing . . . yes, changing into a beak!

"She's done it, Terence! Mother Bloodwort's done it!" cried Belladonna joyfully from the pavilion.

Once more, Mother Bloodwort circled the doomed princess. Then she dismounted and stood back.

"Drat!" said Mother Bloodwort.

For while it was true that she had completely transformed the princess into a bird, that bird was not a swan. It was a duck and, the princess having had trouble with her leg, it was a *lame* duck.

Everybody stared gloomily at the enchanted bird as it waddled, quacking, toward the water. Why there is such a difference between a duck and a swan it is hard to say. There just is. This one seemed to be a Khaki Campbell and not to be at all the sort of person that a prince might fall in love with, recognizing it for the imprisoned soul it was.

But Mother Bloodwort was not daunted. Leaving the duck to stare moodily at a clump of reeds, she took her broomstick back to the fountain and led out the Eastern princess, lovely as an orchid in her shimmering trousers and golden blouse.

"Oi!" moaned Mr. Chatterjee. He had never married, not being sure if his wife would settle in a bottle, and the Princess Shari was all that he desired.

Again the princess followed the old witch meekly; again Mother Bloodwort rode around and around her on her broomstick, reciting her rhyme.

"It's going to work this time," whispered Belladonna to Terence. "Look, the feathers are black! It'll be a lovely swan, you'll see."

They watched, breathless, as Mother Bloodwort slowed down and dismounted.

"I see that I am to be spared nothing," muttered Arriman the Awful, while beside him, Mr. Chatterjee howled with pain.

For the bird now tottering like an overfed alderman toward the lake was a fat, sleek, and foolish-looking penguin.

For a moment, Mother Bloodwort was very much put out. But once more she pulled herself together, and, coughing up a number of dead flies, she re-greased her broomstick and went to fetch the American princess with her pigtail and her T-shirt.

But the princess did not seem to be as hypnotized as the others.

"This is ridiculous," she complained. "What a joke. Make me a black swan or I'll call my lawyer."

But it was not to be. And of all the heartrending things they'd had to watch, one of the worst was seeing a great-great-great-granddaughter of Louis Philippe sitting on a branch and saying in that silly way that budgies have, even in America: "Please give Polly a cracker. Polly wants a cracker, please."

It was Belladonna who knew what was going to happen next. Mother Bloodwort had dropped her broom, her shoulders sagged, her cloud of flies grew silent.

"Don't!" cried Belladonna. "Oh, please, Mother Bloodwort, don't!"

Too late. Already the budgie, looking surprised,

had hopped onto the thing that now stood, four square, upon the path beside the lake.

The ghoul woke and said, "Vomit!" Mr. Chatterjee shook his turbaned head sadly from side to side. And Arriman the Awful rose from his seat.

"No one," he said, "can accuse me of not doing my bit for wizardry and darkness. But there is one thing I will not do and that is *marry a coffee table!*"

And pulling his mantle close about him, the outraged wizard strode away.

CHAPTER 12

ON THE NIGHT BEFORE Madame Olympia was due to do her trick, Terence had a dream. Not a dream, really—a nightmare—a truly horrible one in which he was back at the Sunnydene Home with all the miseries and cruelties he knew so well.

In his dream, Terence was looking for something. Something terribly important, but he didn't know what it was, and growing more and more frantic, he ran through the drab cold rooms, opening battered locker doors, tearing the lids off serving dishes with their soggy dumplings and clammy meatballs, snatching the rough gray blankets from the iron beds. And all the time, as he searched, he heard the sound of laughter—jeering, taunting laughter. Unable to bear it, Terence ran down the mottled steps into the garden.

"I'll find it," said Terence. "I'll find it here."

He bent down and pressed his hands against the gravel, but the laughter was growing louder and more malevolent, and then, suddenly, rearing up in his path, was the dreaded figure of Matron with her sneering lips and baleful eyes, Matron, grown ten foot tall and still trailing the roots which had tethered her—roots which he saw were now made of plaited, bloodstained *human* teeth.

"I *must* find it!" sobbed the little boy.

"You'll never find it! You'll never find it!" screamed Matron. And as her pointed shoe, sharpened to a saw blade, came up to cut him in half, Terence woke.

At first, just finding that he was in his little room at the hall, wearing Mr. Leadbetter's pajama top and miles away from Matron, was a tremendous relief. But this dream was one it didn't seem easy to shake off.

What had he been looking for so desperately? What had Matron said he'd never find? And suddenly, awake, Terence knew what he had not known when he was sleeping.

Rover. It was Rover he'd been looking for.

Only that was silly. Rover was safe in his box. Terence had said good night to him only an hour ago and he'd been in splendid shape, rippling along the rim of the washbasin like an anaconda.

Still, he'd just make absolutely sure. Jumping out of bed, Terence turned on the light and went over to Rover's box, which stood where it always stood, under the window.

He lifted the lid.

"Rover?" he called.

The worm was underground; he usually was, and turning the moist, crumbly earth over with his hands, Terence began to search for his friend.

He was a long way down. And gradually, as he searched, Terence's movements became faster and his breath seemed to stick in his throat.

Even then he didn't panic, but went to fetch a newspaper from the pantry and, spreading the sheets out on the floor, upended Rover's box.

In the thinly spread scattering of earth, the truth could no longer be denied.

Rover was gone.

An hour later, the ogre, the secretary, and Terence were in Mr. Leadbetter's room, desperately deciding what to do. The ogre had rubbed his eye patch onto the back of his head. Mr. Leadbetter was pacing the floor, and Terence, still in the secretary's pajama top, was crouched on the bed like a worried fledgling on a nest.

"I suppose it wouldn't be possible to use another

earthworm for the competition?" said Mr. Leadbetter, coming to rest for a moment.

Terence shook his head. "Belladonna said she'd tried being black sometimes with other worms when I was up at the hall and it didn't work at all. It isn't *any* worm that makes her black; it's Rover."

"But if we got another worm and *told* her it was Rover—" began Mr. Leadbetter, and broke off because he knew he was being silly. Belladonna could tell each ladybird from all its fellows, call a dozen grimy sparrows on a rooftop by their names. It was as foolish to think that all dogs looked alike as it was to imagine that she couldn't tell Rover from every earthworm in the world.

"It's only Friday," said Terence in a rather shaky voice. To him, Rover had not been just a powerful familiar; Terence had lost a dear and valued friend. "It's Madame Olympia's turn tomorrow and Sunday's a free day, isn't it. So by the time Belladonna does her trick on Monday night, don't you think Rover might be"—he gulped and pulled himself together—"might be found?"

The ogre and Mr. Leadbetter exchanged glances. Terence believed that Rover was simply lost, and they thought it was better he went on thinking so. They had their own suspicions, but the boy had quite enough to bear.

"I wouldn't bank on it, son," said Lester, laying his enormous hand on Terence's shoulder.

"I suppose we'll just have to give up all hope of Belladonna winning," said the secretary wearily.

"No!" Terence had jumped from the bed and his voice was strong again. "No! We mustn't give in. Look—Belladonna's just got to win the actual competition, hasn't she? I mean, once Arriman's seen her he's bound to want to marry her and by that time maybe Rover'll have turned up. So can't we *fake* her trick? *Pretend* to have raised Sir Simon?"

"Get someone to impersonate the ghost, do you mean?"

"That's right," said Terence eagerly. "There could be lots of smoke and spotlights and things, like in a pantomime. And then this horrible specter suddenly appearing—*alive!*"

Mr. Leadbetter looked shocked. "That would be cheating, surely?"

Terence turned to him, surprised. "Well, cheating's black, isn't it? And blackness is what Arriman wants."

Mr. Leadbetter saw the logic of this. "But who could we get to take the part of Sir Simon?"

"Ought to be a professional," said Lester. "An actor. I used to know some when I was in the fair, but not now."

"Wait a minute," said Mr. Leadbetter. Now that he

had got used to the idea of cheating, his brain was beginning to tick over once again. "You know my sister Amelia? The one that's Terence's mother and didn't marry the swimming bath attendant?"

The others nodded.

"Well, she keeps a boardinghouse for theatricals in Todcaster. You know, actors and people connected with the stage generally. I wonder if she could find us someone to impersonate Sir Simon?"

"We'll have to move fast," said Lester. "There's only two days and one of them's a Sunday. And I don't really see how I can leave the old man with that Madame Olympia due to do her trick tomorrow."

"And I can't either," said Mr. Leadbetter. "She's asked for some most complicated stuff. Strobe lights and amplifiers and goodness knows what. Oh, dear!"

"*I* can go," said Terence.

There was a pause. Terence had looked wonderfully better since he'd come to the hall, but he was still the smallest and skinniest boy imaginable. And Todcaster was thirty miles away: it meant a train and then a bus into the town.

"Amelia'd look after you," said Mr. Leadbetter slowly. "But . . ." His voice trailed away. He was too polite to say that he didn't think an actor or anyone else would take much notice of Terence.

"Wait a minute," said the ogre. "I've got an idea.

The old man's been making paper money: fivers, ten-ners, the lot. Says he's sick of humping bags of gold around. I'll just go and have a look."

He was back in a few minutes with a large wallet crammed to bursting with notes.

"If you take these you'll be all right," said Lester. "No one'll care a stuff what size you are when they see these. And remember, not a word to Belladonna! She's got to believe that she's really raising Sir Simon and that it's Rover she's touching inside his box. How-ever nutty she is on Arriman, she'll never cheat to get him and that's for sure!"

And then, at last, they went to bed to wait for dawn.

But one light still burnt at Darkington. A single lamp in the window of Madame Olympia's caravan where the enchantress sat gloating over something she held in her cruel, rapacious fingers. Something moist and gentle which, greedy as she was, she prized beyond any jewel.

She had always been certain she would win the com-petition. But now . . . *No one* could beat her now!

152

CHAPTER 13

BELLADONNA WOKE on the morning of Madame Olympia's trick feeling worried and out of sorts. The bloodshot eyeballs on her sleeping bag had gone very pink and fragrant in the night and she had a nasty feeling that they might be turning into the begonias she was so often troubled with. Then there was Mother Bloodwort, who'd been so upset by the budgerigar that not all Belladonna's coaxing could get her to remember the undoing spell for being a coffee table, and Belladonna had had to drag her into her own tent and just hope she'd come round in time. And being Belladonna, she was worried about the flies. Were they all right inside the coffee table; what did they *think*?

But of course she cooked breakfast for the others

and took a cup of tea to Nancy Shouter (who still lay on her camp bed in her vest and knickers telling everyone that it didn't matter which chicken was which) and then she followed Mabel Wrack and Ethel Feedbag up to the hall.

When she reached the steps leading to the south terrace, she met Mr. Leadbetter and the ogre, who told her that Terence had gone into Todcaster to do some errands for Arriman.

"Oh, dear!" said Belladonna. "He'll miss Madame Olympia's trick, and he's so *fond* of magic."

And feeling ridiculously miserable at the thought of spending the day without the little boy, she went to look for the other witches and find a hiding place from which to watch.

Madame Olympia had chosen to do her trick in the underground vaults and cellars of Darkington Hall itself; a cold, dark, echoing warren of passages which opened into a wide cave, as big as several rooms, where in the olden days prisoners had been tortured to death or left to starve. No daylight ever reached this subterranean maze, and as Arriman strode to his place at the judges' table, holding the genie's bottle under his cloak against the cold, he shivered and pulled his collar round his ears.

But when witch number six strode into the cave, his

mood changed. For here, at last, was a witch to be taken seriously.

One moment they were sitting in a dark and gloomy cellar, the next, the cave was aflame with flashing lights that changed from sulfurous yellow to livid green and searing crimson, casting strange and flickering shadows on the walls. Next, the vault was filled with a pulsing, sobbing, shrieking sound as the music of "The Groaning Gizzards," amplified to screaming pitch, pierced the eardrums of the listeners with a song about greed and wretchedness and hate.

Having thus set the stage, the enchantress walked over to the judges' table and bowed low. She was wearing the hood and gown that Arriman had insisted on, but she did not look at all like Mother Bloodwort or Ethel Feedbag or Mabel Wrack. In the secrecy of her caravan, the enchantress had sewn a thousand jet-black sequins onto her gown, which now trembled and glittered in the light of the strobes, as did the rhinestones on the collar and lead of her sinister familiar. Witch number six was tall and carried herself like a queen, and she had looped her necklace of ninety-three molars, fifty-seven incisors, and eleven wisdom teeth so as to make a column of palest ivory round her throat.

"THE SYMPHONY OF DEATH PERFORMED BY A CAST OF THOUSANDS," announced Madame Olympia.

Arriman nodded. He didn't understand a word but it sounded good, and the witch's low, husky voice sent a most agreeable shiver up his spine.

Madame Olympia stepped into the center of the cave. Then she closed her eyes and raised, not her wand, but a whip. A whip like no other in the world. Stolen from an accursed Egyptian tomb, its thongs were made of the plaited skins of human slaves; its lapis lazuli handle had been wrought by an ancient sorcerer so powerful that it had meant death even to know his name.

Three times Madame Olympia laid the whip across the back of the aardvark, charging it with the evil beast's devilish power. Then she cracked the whip—and everybody gasped.

A minute before, the cellar had been empty. Now, from every nook and cranny, from the walls, the ceiling, the floors, from the very air itself, there came tumbling and squeaking and clawing, a hundred, two hundred, five hundred—a thousand huge gray rats.

Not ordinary rats. Lurching, swollen, putrid-eyed rats with scabrous tails and bloated fleas clinging to their matted fur. Rats with death in their filmed eyes— vicious, maddened, *plague-bearing rats!*

Belladonna, hiding behind a pillar, gasped with terror, turned to take Terence's hand, and remembered that he was not there. The ogre said, "Cor!"

and Arriman the Awful leaned forward intently in his seat.

There were so many rats now that they could not all put their diseased and twisted feet on the ground but walked on each other's faces, climbed on each other's backs. . . . And now Madame Olympia turned off the music of "The Groaning Gizzards" and adjusted the amplifier so that it was the squeaks and squeals and hideous scamperings of the rats, magnified beyond bearing, that filled the cave.

Once more she flicked her whip and now, unbelievably, each one of the deformed and frightful animals swelled and swelled . . . grew to twice its size . . . three times. . . . Rats the size of large dogs, now, so that the beasts' heavy scaly tails thumped like hawsers against the stones. And the fleas, those dreaded carriers of bubonic plague, fell off them, large as saucers.

Smiling her cruel, complacent smile, the enchantress watched as the sickening monsters in their thousands filled the cave, pressing each other against the walls, stamping each other underfoot, their whiskers flicking like thongs into the oozing eyes and twitching limbs of their fellows. And still more rats appeared, layer upon layer of them till the cave was filled almost to the roof with the misshapen, screeching monsters.

Only the ghoul was smiling now. The ogre, though the bravest of men, had pulled Mr. Leadbetter away to stand behind Arriman, and the three witches, their differences forgotten, clung together trembling.

Again the enchantress cracked her whip—and they saw that Madame Olympia had not come to the end of her devilry. For even as they watched, the flesh, the hair, the eyes, and skin of the giant rats began to pucker up, to shrivel—and then to vanish altogether till the whole cellar was packed with skeletons. But skeletons which still ran and climbed and fought and bit. Eyeless, hairless, tailless, these were still rats, and on the walls their shadows reared and capered in a grotesque and frightful dance of death.

"Is good, is very good," said Mr. Chatterjee inside his bottle, but he was shaking like a leaf, and Belladonna, almost fainting with disgust, could be glad at least that Terence was not there.

Another crack of the whip, and, lo, the giant rats were clothed in their own flesh again: their gray fur returned, their rheumy eyes, their scabrous tails. But the most horrible part of the trick was still to come. For as they heard the last crack of the whip, all the rats were seized at the same moment with a passionate and uncontrollable desire for *the taste of each other's flesh.* It was cannibalism run riot, cannibalism in its most ghastly form, as the rats sank their yellow teeth into thighs and shoulders and cheeks, and slowly devoured each other—crunch by horrendous crunch.

"I can't bear it," said Belladonna beneath her breath.

There were fewer rats now, and fewer, as more and more twitching bodies vanished into the maws of their fellows. Soon only fifty rats were left, then twenty, then five. . . .

And then one . . . A single, huge rat sitting on its torn haunches in the middle of the floor, blood dripping from a wound in his side, and the still-twitching tail of his neighbor vanishing down his gullet.

Even then it was not quite done. For now this last rat was seized with the most terrible madness of all, and, gasping, the onlookers saw it begin, slowly and relentlessly, to *eat itself.*

Madame Olympia waited till the dripping jaws hung in the air. Then she flicked her whip, the jaws vanished—and she turned to the judges and bowed.

"The Symphony of Death is completed," said Madame Olympia.

And laughed . . .

CHAPTER 14

MADAME OLYMPIA GOT nine out of ten for her "Symphony of Death," as near full marks as could be. The ghoul loved her trick, and though Mr. Chatterjee's teeth went on chattering for a long time inside his bottle, he too thought she was very, very clever. Not even the nastiest caliph in the *Arabian Nights* had done anything more horrible.

"Why did I only give her nine out of ten?" Arriman asked himself that evening. "Why not full marks?" Because it was he who held back. The other two had been willing to go the whole hog and give her that last mark also.

What had prevented him, he wondered? For certainly no witch could touch her for darkness. And the style, the flair! Those strobe lights and that single rat left in the middle of the floor eating its own flesh!

Standing there in his dressing gown, Arriman remembered her low and evil laughter—very attractive it was, really—and that proud toss of the head. No, no one would beat her, that was for sure. There was only one witch to go, and from what he'd heard she was just a little slip of a thing, not to be taken seriously. No, witch number six would be Mrs. Canker, all right. She'd known it herself.

"That was a very fine show today, don't you think, Lester?" he called to the ogre, who was running his bath.

Lester came out of the bathroom looking steamy and rather tired.

"Very fine, sir," he said, his voice expressionless.

"Those flickering lights and the skeletons and those giant fleas. I really liked them, didn't you?"

"Very much, sir."

"Of course, some people would have thought it wasn't necessary to make the rats actually . . . eat each other up like that. I mean, I myself have never gone in much for that sort of thing."

"No, sir."

"But you couldn't have anything blacker. And she was quite good-looking, I think. I didn't see any warts, did you? Or . . . er, whiskers? And I'm almost sure she wasn't wearing Wellies."

"No, she wasn't wearing Wellies, sir."

"So I'm very glad she's won. Well, she's sure to have. Very glad indeed. I think she'll make me an excellent wife. I shouldn't think she'll get things to eat each other very much once we're married. There'll be just straightforward blighting and smiting, wouldn't you say?"

"Yes, sir. Your bath is ready, sir."

"You're not very forthcoming tonight, Lester. What's the matter with you?"

"I'm a little tired, sir."

"Are you? Well, I'll tell you what. Fetch Leadbetter's nephew, Terence. He can scrub my back for me. A nice boy, I'm fond of him."

"I'm afraid he isn't here, sir," said Lester after a short pause. "He's gone to visit . . . his mother."

"Has he? Dear me. That'll be Leadbetter's sister, I suppose. Pity. He'd have enjoyed today, I think," said the magician, untying his dressing gown cord. "Er . . . those were *human* teeth she was wearing round her neck?"

"Undoubtedly, sir."

"Yes. I thought so. It's a new fashion, I suppose. I mean, one must keep up with the times."

Arriman took off his trousers, his socks, and his shoes, and was just about to start on his underpants when the usual plashing sound was heard behind the wainscot.

"Oh, my gawd," said Lester, who was in no mood for Sir Simon.

But before he could make his getaway, the wicked spook came waveringly through the paneling and thrust his pallid, guilty face at Arriman.

"Hello, hello!" said the magician, cheering up as always at the sight of his friend. "I've great news for you. I've found a truly black witch. Looks like a certain winner."

The specter stood in silence, his eye sockets dark and inscrutable.

"I know you aren't into marriage much, but you'll like her. Great style. She did this amazing trick where all these rats . . . ate each other up. Of course, it's not for people with weak stomachs."

Still silent, the specter stood and plashed.

"Oh, blast you!" said Arriman, suddenly furious. "Why don't you *say* something?"

The wizard was in his bath, and Lester, who'd finished scrubbing his back, was out in the corridor talking to Mr. Leadbetter, when a cry of anguish rent the air.

"Lester! Come back! It's trying to get in with me. Take it away!"

Lester did not move.

"Aren't you going to go to him?" asked Mr. Leadbetter.

"Not likely."

"But it's the Kraken. It's trying to get in the bath with him."

"I know it's the Kraken. It always tries to get in the bath with him."

"But—" began Mr. Leadbetter, as another despairing cry came from Arriman.

"Look," said the ogre, rubbing his eye patch. "Last night that bloke sent seven princesses back to seven different countries, and three of them blinking budgies, lame ducks, and penguins before he got to them. A month ago he brought down a ton of toads on the tax inspector's hatchback. What's to stop him sending the Kraken back into the sea or turning him into an umbrella stand or something?"

"You mean he likes being followed about and so on?"

"Likes it?" said the ogre. "He loves it. Laps it up. Can't get enough. You mark my words, if he marries and has a kid he'll be the biggest sucker in the world. Anyone calling that bloke "Daddy" and he's a goner, devilry and wizardry or no."

They both fell silent. The thought of Arriman's marriage lay like a stone on their chests. For Terence hadn't yet returned, and even if he managed to hire an actor, was there really any hope that they'd manage to deceive Arriman?

"Will you stay on if he marries . . . Madame Olympia?" said Mr. Leadbetter, who could hardly bring himself to say the enchantress's name.

Lester shook his craggy head. "Don't think I could," he said. "Goodness knows it goes against the grain to leave the poor bloke, but she really gives me the creeps. I wouldn't put it past her to turn me into a bloomin' baboon *and* get me to nosh meself into the bargain."

"It's the boy I'm worried about," said Mr. Leadbetter. "If anything happens to Terence, Belladonna'll never get over it."

"It won't," said the ogre. "He may be gnat-sized, but he's got a head on his shoulders, that boy. Even now, I wouldn't put it past him to bring home the bacon."

"I do hope you're right, Lester," said the secretary, rubbing his aching tail. "I do very much hope so."

Lester *was* right. No harm had befallen Terence, and midday had found him ringing the doorbell of Amelia Leadbetter's terrace house on the outskirts of Todcaster.

At first when he'd seen again the dreary houses and mean streets of the town he'd been so unhappy in, Terence had felt uneasy and afraid. Ms. Leadbetter's boardinghouse was not far from the Sunnydene Home, and when Terence thought of Matron and her bullying it was as though the last exciting days at Darkington had never been. But then he remembered that he was there to help Belladonna and not to worry about himself, and it was with renewed courage that he rang the bell.

Ms. Leadbetter might not have a tail but she was a brisk and sensible woman, and when she'd read the note her brother had written, and given Terence a cup of tea and a tuna sandwich, she got down to business.

"Now it says here you want an actor to take part in a show up at the hall? Someone tall and used to costume work, is that right?"

Terence nodded. "If he could be used to talking in that old-fashioned way, you know, with 'haths' and 'quothees' and things in it?"

"Shakespearean." Amelia Leadbetter nodded. "Well, there's plenty of unemployed actors around. It's not a comic you want, then? It's straight lead?"

"Oh, yes. He plays a knight in armor. It's a very good part. Sort of a star part."

"And it's got to be someone who can keep a secret. Now, let's see . . . " She leaned across and filled Terence's mug once more with scalding tea. "There's Bert Danby, but he's a boozer and you can never trust a boozer. Then there's Dave Lullingworth—he's down to doing cat food adverts on the telly—but Dave would tell his life story to a brick wall. Wait a minute! I've got it.

Yes, Monty Moon. He's a bit long in the tooth now, but with the right makeup he'll pass. Monty hasn't worked for years, but he was at Stratford once. In fact I'm not sure he didn't play the ghost in Hamlet."

Terence was very excited. "He sounds just right!" he said. An actor who was actually used to playing ghosts was more than he had hoped for.

So Amelia rang up Mr. Moon, who by good luck was at home and agreed to come around immediately.

Monty Moon turned out to be tall and pale and stooped, with a large balding head and a way of tucking in his chin so that it didn't show any sags or wrinkles. When he saw Terence he looked surprised and a little stuffy, but when he saw the wallet Terence had laid casually open on the table he got a lot less stuffy at once.

Five minutes later, they were deep in conversation.

"Now, I understand I'm to play a wicked, wife-

slaying specter who suddenly finds himself brought back to life—is that correct?"

"That's right."

"Now, fill me in, dear boy, fill me in. I must get right *inside* this part. How many wives have I slain? What sort of armor do I wear? Am I bloodstained?"

So Terence told him everything he could think of about Sir Simon, and Mr. Moon wrote it all down in his little notebook.

"And he doesn't wear his helmet or anything," finished Terence. "The top of him is clear and so are his hands so that he can beat his forehead with a plashing sound."

"Like this?" asked Mr. Moon, bringing his arm around in a sweep and striking dramatically at his forehead.

"Well, yes, but it makes a softer noise. Sort of sloshier."

"Don't worry, dear boy. I'll get it right on the night. Now what about the sound effects? Anything special you want when I appear? Howling dogs? Tempests? Crowing cockerels? Just say the word."

They went on discussing things for another hour and deciding what Terence should get ready in the way of skulls, necromancy incense, and so on, for while it had been all right for Belladonna to write "Nothing" on her list when they had Rover to rely on, now that her trick was to be faked, the more props there were, the better. When Mr. Moon heard that he was to get five hundred pounds now and another five hundred if he succeeded in convincing everybody that he was really Sir Simon brought back to life, he promised of his own accord to bring an electrician and a stage manager who had their own van and would help him set the thing up.

"You'll see, dear boy, it'll be a first-rate show. I always did my best work in costume parts. Now just draw a little map for me to show me how we can get into the hall the night before and rig up one or two effects. A trapdoor would have been nice, but one can't have everything."

When they had finished, Terence went to thank Ms. Leadbetter. Returning to say good-bye to Mr. Moon, he found the actor still standing in the middle of the room, bringing his arm in a sweep round to his fore-head, practicing and practicing his plashing sound. And knowing that he had found somebody who took his work seriously, Terence went contentedly away.

CHAPTER 15

$\mathcal{A}$RRIMAN WOKE ON the Sunday before Halloween with a headache. Like Terence, he had had a dream and a dream with teeth in it. He'd seen this necklace floating in the air with five brand-new molars on it: cusps, fillings, and all. Arriman had known at once that they were *his* teeth, and he'd started making teeth-calling noises like the noises you call cows in to be milked with, or chickens to be fed. But the teeth wouldn't come to him; they sort of sneered and floated away—and then Arriman woke and had been almost glad to hear, from under the lid of the soup tureen, the muffled cries of "Daddy! Daddy!" with which the Kraken greeted the dawn.

Mr. Chatterjee was already breakfasting inside his bottle, looking cheerful and relaxed. The climate of the north of England didn't really suit him, and as soon as witch number seven had done her trick he was going to fly home to Calcutta.

"Well, we've got the day free," said Arriman, who was always jolly at breakfast. "Witch number seven's not going to do her trick till tomorrow night. Myself, I think I'll do a little smiting and blighting today; I'm getting short of exercise. What about you, Sniveler?"

But the ghoul, sitting hunched and exhausted over his kidneys, didn't answer. He almost never did.

So Arriman went off and blighted some fir trees and cleft some boulders in twain and called in a thunderstorm from the west—clean, old-fashioned magic which he enjoyed—and thought how nice it had been when the Wizard Watcher had sat peacefully at the gate and his oak trees had not been filled with sleeping grocers and lost witches had not bubbled about in bottomless holes on his east lawn.

"Well, tomorrow it'll all be over," he thought. "Tomorrow I'll know for certain who my wife is going to be. No, I'm being silly. I know *now*."

After which he went to find Mr. Leadbetter to ask him for some milk of magnesia tablets. Magician or no, Arriman had a stomachache.

Meanwhile, down at the campsite, Belladonna sat wretchedly by the campfire, facing the fact that Arriman the Awful was lost to her forever. Even before the enchantress did her trick, Belladonna had not really hoped to win, though when Terence was with her she'd sometimes felt confident and strong. Now, all hope was gone.

She reached for the magic mirror. Arriman was gulping down small white pills. He looked tired and anxious, but what was that to do with her? It would be Madame Olympia now who'd comfort him and smooth the curse curl from his furrowed brow.

Her sad thoughts were interrupted by a fierce rocking noise behind her, followed by a scrabble and a swoosh, and Mother Bloodwort crawled out of Belladonna's tent, her flies sticking like a doormat around her head. The old witch had been a coffee table far too long, and as she collapsed onto the camp stool that Belladonna pulled out for her, she looked very battered and confused.

"What happened?" she asked, blinking. "Was the last one a swan?"

"I'm afraid not," said Belladonna gently. "It was a budgerigar. A very intelligent one. It asked for a biscuit."

"Not the same, though, is it?" the old witch remarked. "Don't know what went wrong. Didn't get a very high mark, I suppose?"

"Well . . . three out of ten. Not bad, really. More than I'll get, anyway."

Mother Bloodwort kicked off her slippers so that the fire could get at her bunions and stared sadly into the flames.

"It wouldn't have made any difference if you'd managed the swan bit," said Belladonna, trying to comfort the old woman. "Because Madame Olympia would have won, anyway. She did this absolutely terrifying thing with rats. The 'Symphony of Death,' it was called. She got nine out of ten: no one can possibly beat her."

"The 'Symphony of Death,' eh?" said Mother Bloodwort thoughtfully. "I've heard of that. Very black, that is, *very* nasty. There's not too many witches could do that even in my day. I should think she'd gobble up poor Arriman as soon as look at him. Good job he's got nice teeth."

"Oh, no, *no*! Don't say that!" cried Belladonna. "Arriman's the mightiest wizard in the world! She couldn't hurt him, she couldn't!"

"Oh, well, maybe not," said Mother Bloodwort. She sighed. "I suppose marriage wouldn't really have suited me. I've lost the habit, I reckon, and that turning-myself-young-again spell doesn't seem to be up to much."

She got up creakingly, went to fetch her tin with the coronation on the lid, and began to shake her head into it, blowing on the flies as they fell to change them into maggots. "Best be getting ready for lunch, I suppose."

But before Mother Bloodwort could move, Ethel Feedbag and Mabel Wrack came lurching up to them, both heaving with rage.

"Look!" said Mabel, putting down the bucket in which she was taking Doris for her midday stroll and pointing with a shaking arm at the enchantress's caravan.

"Stuck-up, snooty cow!" raged Ethel Feedbag.

Belladonna looked up, frowning.

"How strange," she said.

Madame Olympia's caravan was the kind with a little stove and a chimney. And of course, as she was a witch, the smoke from her chimney was blowing against the wind. But that wasn't what had made Ethel and Mabel so mad. Madame Olympia had magicked the smoke so that it came out in letters: the letter *O* followed by the letter *C* again and again, standing out as clear as could be against the deep blue sky of autumn.

"What does it mean?" asked Belladonna, puzzled.

"What do you think it means?" snarled Mabel Wrack. "Those are her new initials, of course. Olympia Canker. She's letting us all know she's won."

"But she hasn't won! She *hasn't*!"

The voice was a new one, and Belladonna, hearing it, sprang to her feet.

175

"Terence! Oh, I'm so glad you're back! You've no idea how much I've missed you."

But though he hugged her as lovingly as always, Terence's mud-colored eyes were fixed on the enchantress's chimney and his jaw was set.

"You're going to beat her, Belladonna. You're going to get ten out of ten tomorrow. You'll see!"

CHAPTER 16

IN THE GREAT HALL at Darkington, the clock struck eleven. An hour till the true beginning of Halloween, the Feast of the Dead, when the shades of the departed draw closer, for a few dread hours, to those they have left behind.

In a dozen sconces, the tall candles burnt with a sickly flame; logs of gnarled and knotted alderwood, like ancient severed limbs, hissed and spat in the grate, and the wind, howling through the rafters, eerily stirred the tapestry of the gentleman being shot with arrows while burning at the stake.

Belladonna, waiting for her turn, was as white as a sheet under her gown and mask. Terence had taken her through her trick again and again. He'd told her that everything would be ready, laid out on a great refectory table covered with a cloth, and that he himself would be hiding underneath it, ready to hand her Rover at the right moment and prompt her if she forgot anything. And waiting behind a tall embroidered screen with the other witches, she could see that he'd been as good as his word. The table, with its candlesticks, its grinning skull, and portrait of Sir Simon, looked just like one of those dreadful necromancy altars she'd seen in books. But that only made her more horribly afraid of the deed she was about to do.

"Witch number seven—step forward!" commanded Mr. Leadbetter.

The secretary was looking tired and careworn. However much he argued with himself, it seemed to him that cheating was *not* the same as wizardry and darkness. Cheating, whichever way you looked at it, was *mean.* And what if Monty Moon let them down and all they'd done was make Belladonna look a fool?

But Belladonna, trying to stop her knees from trembling, was walking toward the judges' table, and, pulling himself together, Mr. Leadbetter said:

"Announce your trick!"

Belladonna turned and bowed low to the judges. Her voice shook a little on the first words, but she lifted her head bravely and her clear young voice reached even to the farthest corner of the hall.

"I AM GOING TO BRING SIR SIMON MONTPELIER

BACK FROM THE DEAD," said Belladonna, allowing herself a lingering look at Arriman as he sat, brooding and a little bored, between the other judges.

But at her words, the magician leaned forward, furiously frowning, and a spurt of fire burst from his left ear. Going to do necromancy, was she? A deed so difficult that he, Arriman the Awful, had failed at it again and again. A little slip of a witch, not up to his shoulder. How *dared* she?

For a moment, it looked as though Arriman was going to make a scene. But even as he brought his fist down, ready to bang it on the table, his curiosity got the better of him. It was impertinence, of course, the most appalling cheek. Still, it wouldn't hurt to let her try. Perhaps she had guessed how achingly he longed for his plashing, ghostly friend.

So Belladonna stepped forward to the table with its long cloth and candlesticks and skull, and as she did so, Terence slipped Rover's closed box into the pocket of her gown. Then she took a pin from her other pocket and, jabbing it into her finger, let a drop of blood fall, like a red pearl, into the incense pot. And immediately there was a flash, and a sheet of rose and amethyst and orange smoke rose almost to the roof.

"Thank gawd," said Lester, who believed that if you had to cheat it was best to cheat good and proper. He'd heard a van drive into the courtyard at dawn, but that was the only sign of Monty Moon and his crew, and he'd begun to have doubts.

"Let there be darkness!" said Belladonna. And instantly, every candle guttered and went out, and the hall was plunged into inky impenetrable night.

Belladonna let the darkness and silence stay there for a moment, making everyone's flesh crawl a little. Then she took up the hollow skull and walked over to the magic triangle that Terence had chalked out for her below the tapestry.

"Do you hear me, shades of the underworld?" cried Belladonna, raising the skull.

They heard her. First came a low and fearful murmuring which swelled to a cacophony of cackling, screaming, and screeching, and under the table, Terence sighed with relief. Mr. Moon had been as good as his word—and better.

Belladonna's teeth were chattering badly now. It seemed that Terence was right and that with Rover to help her there was no limit to her darkness. But she went on bravely, and putting down the skull, she fetched the portrait of Sir Simon and held it aloft.

"I call upon thee, shades, to release from eternal torment the spirit of this man!" she intoned.

More screams and yells from the spirits, while in the rafters, the ravens hideously croaked.

"Sir Simon Montpelier, Knight of Darkington, I command thee to appear!" cried Belladonna.

The jabbering and screeching died away, and now, in the black silence of the hall, there appeared a series of white, disembodied lights which bobbed and flickered, giving off at the same time an almost unendurable stench of decay.

"Corpse candles," murmured Mother Bloodwort, drawing her skirt away from one which had come too close.

Then, all in the same second, the corpse candles went out, and over the hall there spread a coldness such as they had never before experienced: the coldness of the tomb, the grave, of death itself.

"I wonder how he did that?" murmured Lester, whose respect for Mr. Moon was growing every minute. "Some sort of chemical, I suppose."

But now the coldness was passing and everyone's gaze was drawn upward to the wall on the left of the chimney breast. For the tapestry of the man stuck with arrows while burning at the stake was beginning to glow and shine and shimmer with a most unearthly light.

Belladonna felt in her pocket for a last squeeze of Rover's box. She was incredibly tired and her knees felt like water, but she wouldn't weaken now. And taking up a wand from the table, she struck the ground thrice and, prompted by Terence, who had been whispering the spells with her all along, she said the words that are older than any book of magic in the world:

"*Allay fortission! Fortissio Roa!*" cried Belladonna.

The glow around the tapestry grew stronger. The clock struck midnight. And as the last chime died away, there crept around the edge of the hanging, slowly and gropingly—a hand. A white hand, limp and long-fingered, with an emerald riding one knuckle.

For a few moments, the hand just hung there. Then it felt for the sides of the tapestry and with a sudden violent gesture, tore it from the wall and threw it on the ground.

And there stepped from the stone recess—wan and weary, but definitely alive—the figure of an Elizabethan knight.

A shriek of joy from Arriman broke the stunned silence.

"Sir Simon! Is it really you?" he cried, pushing

back his chair so hard that it crashed to the ground. And dashing forward he seized the specter's hands in his own.

"Aye, 'tis I," intoned Sir Simon. His voice was high and reedy, like an oboe playing something sad. "Ye see before ye the guilty, tainted flesh of Sir Simon Montmorency Montpelier."

"Oh, I can't believe it! But yes, yes, I can feel you; you're solid! And look at that vein throbbing in your left temple! Oh, happy, happy day! What ecstasy! What bliss!"

Sir Simon removed his left hand from Arriman's grasp and brought it up to his forehead. The plashing sound was much, much better than when he'd been a ghost: more solid, wetter, in every way more *real*.

Arriman was quite overcome. "The talks we'll have! The confidences! The walks! The delights of nature we will share! My dear, dear fellow, this is the best day of my life!"

Then, remembering at last that this was a competition, Arriman turned to the other judges.

"Ten out of ten, gentlemen, are we agreed?"

The ghoul nodded—he'd have liked the whole world to be inhabited by people who were dead—and kind Mr. Chatterjee smiled.

But these words were never heard by Belladonna. Overcome by fatigue, terror, and strain, Belladonna had fainted.

CHAPTER 17

BELLADONNA WOKE IN a four-poster bed in a room at the very top of the north tower at Darkington. Mr. Leadbetter and the ogre had carried her there after the end of the competition, while Terence hopped round her, worrying about her and congratulating her at the same time. Belladonna couldn't remember much about it now; only that she'd been anxious about the baby rabbits and about not having a toothbrush, and that Terence had said he'd go down to the campsite and see to everything.

How long ago had that been, she wondered. It still seemed to be dark, but now she felt refreshed and very happy. She'd done it! She'd won! She was to be the bride of Arriman, to be with him always, to stroke his mustache and massage his ankles if they swelled and share his secrets, his hopes, and his fears.

"Oh, glory!" said Belladonna, and smiling, fell asleep once more.

But a *happy* white witch, a white witch blissfully in love, can be a disaster. While Belladonna slept the room began to fill with exquisite saucer-sized snowflakes, each a perfect, six-pointed star, and the flakes did not melt but alighted softly on the hangings of the bed, the embroidered rug, the washstand. An enameled musical box burst from the chest of drawers and began to play a dreamy Viennese waltz; strings of gold and silver tinsel draped themselves across the ceiling, and the windowsills filled with rows of crystal goblets brimful of Knickerbocker Glories.

But Belladonna, knowing nothing of all this, slept on.

While Belladonna lay dreaming in the tower room, Arriman sat in the library talking to Sir Simon Montpelier. Arriman had suggested that the knight might like to slip into something more comfortable than the breastplate and leg armor he had worn for four hundred years, and though he'd murmured something about his underclothes not being quite the thing, the wife-slayer was now wearing Arriman's second-best dressing gown—a maroon one appliquéd with fiends and pitchforks—and was telling the magician the story of his life.

"So the Lady Anne was the first of your wives?" inquired Arriman, pushing the whisky decanter toward his friend.

"Even so," agreed Sir Simon. "She was the one I drowned. Ere the cock crew thrice, I drowned her. I had to. She madeth the sleeping chamber rumble as if cleft in twain."

"Ah! She snored, you mean?" said Arriman. "Very distressing, that. Nothing worse."

The knight nodded and plashed a little.

"Then I wedded the Lady Mary. Her I took by the throat and fastened my foul fingers around."

"Strangulation." Arriman nodded.

"She hath cheateth me of my victuals," said the knight.

"Fiddled the housekeeping, did she? In that case she deserved everything she got. And the next one?"

"Next I espoused the fair Olivia. Her I walled up in the privy for looking with favor upon the knave who emptied of her slops."

Arriman shook his head. "Terrible, terrible. What you've been through!"

Sir Simon went on to tell the magician about the Lady Julia, whom he'd stabbed in the buttery because she had a horrid little dog that yapped, and the Lady Letitia, whom he'd thrown over a cliff because she guzzled, and he was just about to start on the Lady Henrietta, whom he'd knocked off with a poisoned halibut because she drove him nutty walking in her sleep, when there was a knock at the door and the ogre entered.

"The Kraken's in his tureen waiting for you to say good night, sir, and I've laid out your pajamas. Is there anything else you require?"

"No, no, Lester, that's fine. You can go to bed."

"I've put Sir Simon in the green room," said Lester, winking at Mr. Moon, "on account of it being handy for the bathroom, like."

"Good, good," said the magician impatiently. There was still one more wife to go and he wanted to hear about her.

"There was a postcard from the Wizard Watcher by the late post, sir," the ogre continued. "It has reached Skegness and hopes to be back the day after tomorrow."

He had got through to the magician at last. "Now that is good news! I'm really glad about that. I wouldn't have liked it to miss the wedding."

But the word "wedding" had a bad effect on Arriman. His brooding face darkened and he drained his whisky in a single desperate gulp. "You've no idea what women do, Lester. Sir Simon's been telling me. They snore and have little dogs and walk in their sleep. And those are just *ordinary* women! I mean, this witch . . . she must be really very black to do necromancy. I should think a witch as black as that would have some pretty nasty habits."

"Not necessarily, sir," said Lester.

"And if she's blacker than me . . . I mean, I don't want to be *henpecked*. I can't imagine anything sillier than a henpecked wizard."

"Sir," said Lester, losing his patience, "you haven't even *seen* witch number seven. And anyway, what about your duty to wizardry and darkness? What about this blighting black baby you're going to have? What," said Lester, "did we have this blinking contest *for*?"

The magician sighed. "Yes, yes, you're quite right, Lester. I'll go and see her first thing in the morning and fix the date."

As Lester left the room, Arriman was leaning forward eagerly and saying: "And the last one? The Lady Beatrice, wasn't it? What did she do?"

"Smelled," said Sir Simon gloomily. "Most vilely and horribly hath she smelled."

And having come to the end of his wives, the knight poured himself another whisky and began again at the beginning.

Arriman kept his word, and the next morning saw him climbing the curved steps to Belladonna's tower.

The magician wasn't feeling too good. Sir Simon had told him about his murdered wives not once but three times, and though Arriman understood how much the wife-slayer needed to talk after four hundred years of only plashing, he did feel very tired. Nor were the ogre and the secretary, following close behind him, exactly full of beans. They'd spent the night worrying in case the real Sir Simon burst clanking through the paneling and gave the game away, and they didn't really like the way Monty Moon was settling into his part. That was the trouble with actors. You could get them *on*stage, but getting them off was another matter.

"Leadbetter, you wouldn't lie to me," said Arriman, turning round. "Is she covered in warts? I mean, *covered*?"

"No, sir. Not at all."

"What about her fingers and toes? All there, are they? No . . . stumps, for example? Nothing webbed or anything? Nothing *clawed*?"

"No, sir."

The magician climbed a few more steps and turned again.

"And . . . er . . . nothing personal, you understand, because yours is charming. I mean, it's part of you, but it could be awkward in a wife. In short, Leadbetter, has she got . . . a tail? You know, one of those forked jobs, a bit black and bushy?"

"No, sir," said the secretary. "Witch number seven is tailless."

"And her name is Belladonna?"

"That's right."

"Belladonna Canker. Ah, well."

And reaching the top step, Arriman paused, took a deep breath—and threw open the door.

Belladonna was sitting up in bed. The sun, streaming through the east window, had turned her hair into a shower of gold; her eyes were bright with happiness and blue as a summer sky, and she was singing a sweet and foolish little song: the kind with roses in it and springtime and love. Rather a lot of love.

Arriman stood stock-still in the doorway, unable to move.

"Who . . . is this?" he stammered.

"That is Belladonna, sir. Witch number seven. The winner of the contest!"

"You're not pulling my leg?"

"No, sir."

"She's not . . . er . . . in an enchanted state? I mean, she hasn't taken on another shape just to bamboozle me? She looks like that all the time?"

"All the time, sir."

Belladonna, meanwhile, was gazing rapturously at Arriman, her heart in her eyes. This was the closest she had ever been to him, and she was drinking in the flaring nostrils, the tufty ears, the curve of his noble nose.

"Belladonna!" said the magician, stepping forward. His voice throbbed, his eyes burnt, and his chest heaved like a pair of bellows.

"Arry?" murmured Belladonna shyly, from beneath lowered lashes.

"Arry! All my life I've wanted someone to call me Arry."

Lester and Mr. Leadbetter exchanged glances. Things were turning out exactly the way they'd hoped, but they hadn't reckoned on being quite so embarrassed.

"Leadbetter, we must be married at once! Tomorrow at the latest!" said Arriman, who was now sitting on Belladonna's bed and grasping both her hands.

Mr. Leadbetter sighed. It was just like Arriman to spend weeks grumbling about having to get married and then fall in love like a ton of bricks and make trouble for everyone.

"I'm afraid that's impossible, sir. There are the wedding invitations to be sent, the food to be ordered, the bride's clothes to be bought. Three weeks is the shortest I can manage it in."

"Three weeks! I can't wait three weeks! Can you wait three weeks, my pretty?"

"Oh, my gawd," murmured Lester. He had forgotten how absolutely ridiculous people sounded when they were in love.

But now at last the really peculiar look of the tower room had got through to Arriman, and without letting go of Belladonna's hands, he looked with surprise at the exquisite snowflakes, the strings of gold and silver tinsel, the shimmering moonstones now dripping from the mouth of the wash jug.

Catching every movement of her beloved's eyes, Belladonna flushed and said: "I'm sorry about all this. It happened while I was asleep. You see, Arry, I feel I should tell you that I used to be white."

"No, no, my treasure," said the magician dotingly.

"That's quite impossible. Your hair is so golden, your cheeks are so pink, your eyes are such a lovely, lovely blue."

"I don't mean that," said Belladonna. "I mean, my *magic* was white. I was a white witch."

She had got through to Arriman at last. A spasm crossed his face. "My dearest love, you mustn't *say* such things!"

"Oh, it's all right. I'm not white now. I'm very, very black. Well, you saw how black I was. *Rover* made me—" She broke off with a little cry. "Oh, how dreadful of me! How selfish and cruel! I left Rover in his match-box all night! Oh, poor, poor Rover; he'll be so dry and sad—Terence will never forgive me."

She had freed her hands from Arriman's and, jumping out of bed, ran to the chair where her gown was lying.

"Here it comes!" whispered the ogre.

Belladonna had found the matchbox, had opened it, was staring at it while the color drained from her face.

When she spoke it was in a voice so full of anguish and disbelief that they hardly recognized it.

"Rover's gone," said Belladonna. "He's *gone!*"

There was a long and dreadful pause. "I have to find him, Arry, I have to. He's my familiar, you see. Without him, I'm nothing."

She began to search desperately, lifting up the Knickerbocker Glories, pushing aside the snowflakes. Arriman had started to help her when he saw the ogre beckoning to him from the other side of the room.

"Sir," said Lester, when he'd got his master outside the door. "It's my belief that it ain't no good looking because that worm ain't lost. He's been stolen. I've thought so all along."

"All along? But Belladonna's only just noticed that he's gone," said Arriman, looking puzzled.

Lester saw that he'd made a mistake. If he told Arriman that Rover had been gone before the raising of Sir Simon, he'd get suspicious at once. Belladonna had made it clear that her blackness came from Rover, so if there was no Rover there was no blackness, and that led right back to Sir Simon not being Sir Simon at all but an actor called Monty Moon.

"I can't go into that now, sir," he said. "But I can tell you one thing. Rover may be a good performer, but he's not up to shutting a matchbox after he's crawled out of it. No, that worm's been nicked and I'll bet my bottom dollar I know who did it."

"Who?"

"Witch number six. That Madame Olympia. Leadbetter thinks the same."

"Oh, no! Surely not!" Arriman was very shocked. "The one with the interesting, cruel smile and the . . . er . . . rats?"

Lester nodded. "And if I'm right we ought to be getting down to her caravan quick. The witches are due to go back tomorrow."

Arriman was frowning. The more he remembered the "Symphony of Death," the more he thought it would be better not to meet the enchantress head-on.

"I think we'd better take her by surprise," he said. "And that means disguises. How would you like to be a rabbit, Lester?"

"Not at all, sir."

"Oh, come on! Be a sport!"

"No, sir. Absolutely and definitely, *no.*"

While Arriman and the ogre were talking, Madame Olympia was packing her things.

Since Belladonna had won the competition, the enchantress had been in such a towering rage that she had made three holes in the floor of the caravan where she had stamped her feet. She had also come out in a rash from sheer temper, and it was this which made her decide to go back to London immediately, to her beauty parlor, where she could mix some creams and ointments to get rid of it. Then she planned to come back like the queen in *Snow White* with a poisoned apple or some poisoned stays which she would sell to Belladonna at the door and which would kill her. Except that probably Belladonna did not *wear* stays— people did not seem to nowadays—so she would have to think of something else.

So now she came out of the caravan to do one last job, and that was to throw some rubbish she did not want onto the fire. Some nasty, useless, disappointing rubbish that she wanted to get rid of once and for all. And as she did so, a rabbit and a fox ran between her legs and bounded into the caravan.

If she had bothered to look, she might have noticed that the fox was an unusually handsome one with a great bushy autumn-colored tail, and that the rabbit, which looked cross, had only a single eye. But she only turned round furiously and said: "Get out at *once*, you dirty animals. Shoo!"

But of course they weren't dirty animals anymore.

Sitting at the table were Arriman the Awful and the ogre.

"Good morning," said Arriman, polite as always.

"How dare you!" screamed the enchantress. "How *dare* you break in like this?"

Arriman looked at her. An enchantress's power is useless on someone who is truly in love. Arriman could see her now as she really was and he did not like what he saw.

"We believe you may have something that belongs to my fiancée," said the magician. "Her familiar, to be exact."

"Her familiar? What on earth are you talking about? I've a perfectly good familiar of my own, as you can see." Madame Olympia kicked the cowering aardvark with the heel of her shoe.

Then she shut her eyes and began to gabble something under her breath. But before she could get any further, Lester, following a signal from his master, had taken the full milk jug and upended it over the enchantress's head.

"*Phloo,*" spluttered Madame Olympia. "*Guggle!*"

Milk is a well-known antidote to magic, almost as good as eating roses or holding a rowan twig.

"Quick! Search the caravan!" ordered Arriman, while the enchantress, groping for a towel, used some words that even Lester had not heard before.

So they searched the caravan, turning out the built-in cupboards, opening Madame Olympia's half-packed suitcase, feeling under the bed.

Nothing. Not a sign of Rover.

"You see," jeered the enchantress. "Turn the caravan inside out for all I care."

She flung herself out of the caravan and, picking up the little bundle of rubbish, walked with a gleeful smile toward the fire.

It was Arriman who caught on first and ran after her, the ogre following.

"Stop! Stop! Let's see what you're burning."

"Never!" shouted the enchantress, and laughed.

Then she brought her arm over in an arc and threw her bundle onto the flames.

Arriman did not stop for any of the spells that would have made him fireproof, or any magic words that would have doused the flames. Instead, he plunged his hand into the red-hot blaze and drew out the crumpled bundle just as it had begun to catch.

And there—dry and bewildered-looking at the bottom of a cornflake packet—was Rover!

Belladonna, sitting wistfully in a chair in the tower room, greeted the earthworm with a shriek of joy. But then she saw the magician's hand.

"Oh, Arry! You're hurt! How dreadful!"

And she took his hand and bent over it and began to croon one of her wholeness songs about the beauty of new skin and the cleverness of having five fingers, and almost at once, the pain disappeared and the blisters also.

"My angel! My little blossom! You've healed me!" cried Arriman, growing more and more besotted.

"Yes, but that was the *old* me," said Belladonna hastily. "The new me is quite different, Arry. If you give me Rover, I'll show you."

The ogre handed her the worm, which he'd damped down and fettled up with some moist earth as they came.

"What would you like, Arry?" she said. "Shall I turn the tinsel into some moldering thighbones, perhaps? Sort of in a crisscross pattern? And what about making the snowflakes into gaping wounds? You do *like* gaping wounds?"

"I adore them, my angel. They're almost my favorite thing."

So Belladonna closed her eyes while the ogre and Mr. Leadbetter and Arriman stood and watched.

The next half hour was one that none of them ever forgot. Belladonna worked and she worked and she worked, not once letting the strain and puzzlement show on her face. But at the end of the time, she put down Rover and threw herself with a wail of anguish onto the bed.

"It's hopeless!" she cried. "Quite, quite hopeless. You must forget me, Arry. You must wed another. My blackness has absolutely and completely gone!"

The others looked round the room once more. The strings of gold and silver tinsel were still there, but between them there sparkled a chain of most delightful fairy dolls. In the center of each exquisite, still unmelted snowflake shone a diadem of flawless pearls. But it was the pots of pink and rather blobby flowers which had sprung up all over the place that made Lester's voice, when he spoke, sound like a voice from the tomb.

"Begonias," said the ogre, shaking his gigantic head. "Bloomin' *begonias.*"

It was in this moment of complete despair that Arriman showed himself a most true and noble lover.

"My angel!" he said, gathering Belladonna into his arms. "What does it matter? You can fill the whole place with Knickerbocker Glories and those . . . er . . . pink blobby things, and it wouldn't matter to me. All I care about is you!"

But though she let her head rest for a moment on his manly shoulders, Belladonna was firm.

"No, Arry; you have a duty. Remember what the competition was about? 'Darkness is All,' you said. Suppose we had—" Her voice broke but she pulled herself together. "Suppose we had a white baby? Or even a gray baby? What could a baby like that do with a devilish maze and a fiendish laboratory and all the other lovely things you've worked so hard to make? How could a white baby keep wizardry and darkness alive in the land? You don't just belong to yourself, Arry. You belong to all the doom and dastardry and devilment in the world, and I'd never forgive myself if I let you forget what was right."

And nothing that the desperate wizard could say would shake her.

"I'll go as soon as I can get my things together," she said, keeping her voice steady with an effort. "If I'm so white that I can ruin a powerful familiar like that, the farther away I am the better. Only I must say good-bye to Terence and give Rover back to him." She turned to Mr. Leadbetter and the ogre who were standing miserably by the door. "By the way, where *is* Terence? I haven't seen him for ages."

The ogre frowned. "He wasn't at the campsite," he said.

"Are you sure?" said Mr. Leadbetter sharply. "He said he was going down to the campsite to get Belladonna's things and help the witches clear up. I was sure he'd spent the night down there. You know what boys are with tents."

And, their great sorrow laid aside for a moment, they all looked at each other with a new anxiety.

Where *was* Terence?

CHAPTER 18

TERENCE, AT THAT MOMENT, was locked in a small dark room with high barred windows in the place he feared and hated more than any other in the world. For the worst thing that could have happened to Terence had happened. Matron had come unrooted; she sent out an alarm; he'd been recaptured as he ran across the road to go to the campsite, and now he was back in the home.

It had happened so suddenly that he'd had no chance to defend himself. A police car had been waiting outside the gates (even policemen didn't dare to go *inside* the gates at Darkington). Two men had stepped out of the car and grabbed him, and before he knew where he was, he was inside the car and driving at seventy miles an hour back to Todcaster.

The policemen had been quite kind, only telling

him what a stupid thing it was to run away: children were always caught in the end, they said. Apparently a tradesman who delivered groceries to the home had seen Terence at the station on the day he went to find Ms. Leadbetter and had noticed him buying a ticket back to Darkington.

But if the policemen had been fatherly enough, Matron had received the woebegone little boy with a gloating triumph. She said nothing about the rooting; most probably she had forgotten it (there is often loss of memory after rooting), but she had not forgotten her grudge against Terence. And now, after a night spent on a lumpy mattress with only a bowl of claggy porridge for his breakfast, he was waiting for her to come and punish him.

The door opened and Matron entered. She was yellower and more like a camel than ever, and she began at once: "Now then, what are we going to do with you? Beat you? Send you to Borstal? Keep you locked up for good?"

On she went, scolding and threatening, while Terence cowered against the wall and wondered why God hadn't given people earlids as well as eyelids so that they could shut out such dreadful sounds. And all the while, his anxious thoughts raced back to Darkington. Had Belladonna noticed yet that Rover had gone? Had Arriman learned that Sir Simon was a fake? Would anyone miss him and try to find him or would they think he'd run away because he didn't like it at the hall? No, they couldn't think that; they *couldn't.*

Matron was still standing over him, shouting and blustering, the stream of ugly words pouring out of her mouth like pitch. She'd have liked to hit Terence, to knock him against the wall, but there were stupid health inspectors who came round these days and made trouble. One had actually had the nerve to tell her that her methods were old-fashioned. Still, there were plenty of things you could do that didn't leave marks. A pinch under the wrist, for example. Matron had a special line in pinches.

"So just you remember, my boy. One squeak out of you, one more bit of trouble and you'll stay in this room for the rest of your life, do you understand?"

Terence nodded. In the few hours since he'd been back at the home, all his sparkle and bounce had gone. Terence could stand the blackest magic and enjoy it, but unkindness and spite just finished him.

And so the grayness and misery of the home closed over Terence once again. By the time he'd eaten his boiled fish and black-eyed potatoes at the scrubbed dining table, had his fingernails inspected, and put on his mackintosh for the boring walk they always took when there was no school—past the Formica factory, left at the gasworks, and back down a long road of seedy terrace houses—he'd almost forgotten that only a few hours ago life had been an exciting and wonderful thing.

But just as the line of children, led by the assistant matron, a watery lady called Ms. Kettle, was crossing the road back to the home, a strange thing happened. Terence heard his name called and, looking up, he saw Ms. Leadbetter carrying a shopping basket and waving her umbrella.

"Wait!" she shouted. "I want to speak to you!"

She marched up to Terence, ignoring Ms. Kettle, who was wittering away at the head of the line, and said: "Just the person I wanted to see. Though what you're doing here, I don't know. I thought you were staying with my brother."

"I was," said Terence. "But they caught me." He looked up at her eagerly. "If you could tell Mr. Leadbetter I'm here, *please.* I don't want him to think—"

"Come along, Terence Mugg. No loitering," called Ms. Kettle sharply.

But Ms. Leadbetter, who had once thrown a drunken actor down three flights of stairs, was not at all cowed by Ms. Kettle.

"What I was going to say," she said, bending down and speaking quickly into Terence's ear, "was that I've just had a message from the hospital. From poor

Monty Moon. He's so sorry he's had to let you down. It was the van—the one belonging to the electrician. Monty says the tires were worn to a shred, but he wouldn't listen. Anyway, they ran into a ditch on the way to Darkington and the whole lot of them were taken to the hospital. Just cuts and bruises, but poor Monty didn't really come round till this morning. It was last night, wasn't it, that he was supposed to do the show?"

Terence was looking at her in amazement.

"Yes," he said. "It was last night. But he didn't let us down. He did do the show. He was there."

"No, he wasn't. Not Monty. He's been in the hospital since Sunday and the stage manager and electrician with him. He never got to Darkington at all. That's what's worrying him, on account of having taken the five hundred pounds."

But now Ms. Kettle had had enough. She left the front of the line, yanked Terence by the arms, and marched him away.

Terence made no move to resist. He had too much to think about.

If Monty Moon had never got to Darkington, who had appeared from behind the tapestry? Who was the Elizabethan knight they had "raised"? Could it be . . . didn't it *have* to be . . . Sir Simon Montpelier himself?

So Belladonna had really done it! But Rover hadn't been there, that was certain. The box Terence had handed Belladonna was empty. And without Rover, Belladonna was absolutely white.

Where had all that darkness come from, then? What did it mean?

"Take your coat off, you lazy boy, and don't stand there dreaming," said Ms. Kettle, who took her tone from Matron.

Terence didn't even hear.

The afternoon darkened. The children had beans on toast. Ms. Kettle read them a story from *Struwelpeter* about a boy who had his thumbs cut off, and then they all trooped up to bed. Lying in his iron cot, looking at the same crack in the ceiling that he'd looked at for years and years, Terence heard Billy, in the next bed, begin to snuffle and cry.

"What is it, Billy?" asked Terence.

"I'm thirsty; I want a drink."

"Well, why don't you go and get one?"

"I'm scared," said Billy. He was partly deaf and wet his bed and was always in trouble too.

"I'll go," said Terence.

He slipped out of bed and tiptoed out into the corridor toward the bathroom. Matron and Ms. Kettle were talking in the hall below—and they were talking about him.

"Of course, he is a troublemaker," Ms. Kettle agreed. "But I've always felt, Matron, that you dislike him particularly."

"Dislike him? Of course I dislike him. And I've every reason to. Look!"

She held up her hand, and Ms. Kettle peered at it.

"The little finger, do you mean?"

"Yes," shouted Matron. "The little finger I do mean. The little finger that Terence Mugg bit to the bone and mutilated when he was brought to me, a babe in arms, and I bent over to say 'Ickle bickle boo' to him as I do to all my babies. Even now I get shooting pains in it when I knit."

"Goodness," said Ms. Kettle. "And he was only three weeks old, wasn't he, when they brought him from the kiosk? Most unusual!"

"Everything about that horrible child is unusual. He gives me the creeps. Do you know, whatever you do to him, he never cries? Never. He'll sit there with his eyes like saucers and he'll wince with pain, but he's never shed a tear in all the time he's been here. It's unnatural, that's what it is, and I'll knock it out of him, see if I don't!"

A sharp noise from the top of the stairs made them both turn round. Terence was standing on the landing in his pajamas. He was standing perfectly still, as though in a state of shock, and the glass of water he'd been fetching for Billy lay in splinters at his feet.

"How *dare* you, Terence Mugg! How *dare* you get out of bed! Just you wait, you've gone too far this time. You've gone too far!"

Terence waited. He felt very queer. There was a sort of roaring in his ears and the landing felt as though it were rocking and swaying beneath his feet.

Matron was on the first step . . . the second. . . . Now she was almost up to him, her arms outstretched to get him by the shoulders and shake him.

Terence took a long deep breath. He closed his eyes. . . .

CHAPTER 19

THE WIZARD WATCHER, returning from a holiday it hadn't enjoyed at all, arrived at Darkington the following morning, and as all three heads agreed, it was like coming back to a blinking funeral.

Arriman and Belladonna sat hopelessly entwined on the big sofa in the black drawing room, gazing into each other's eyes. Belladonna had packed her straw basket and folded her tent and was only waiting for Terence to be found before going away forever to a life of loneliness, begonias, and pain.

Except that it was beginning to look as though Terence never *would* be found. Mr. Leadbetter (who'd quite forgotten that the little boy was not really his nephew) had rung every hospital in the district in case there'd been an accident, but no one had news of him and the anxiety was dreadful.

Meanwhile the Kraken wasn't exactly helping by tottering back and forth saying "Daddy!" to Arriman and "Mummy!" to Belladonna and making both of them extremely wet. Nor did the wife-slayer take any notice of the fact that everyone was so upset, but plashed up and down droning on about how he'd smothered Lady Beatrice, strangled Lady Mary, and knocked off Lady Henrietta with a halibut.

It was to this scene of misery that the Wizard Watcher returned, and it made no bones about saying that it wasn't the sort of homecoming it had expected.

Not that Arriman wasn't terribly pleased to see it; he was, and immediately introduced Belladonna, whom the monster took to at once.

"Very nice," said the Middle Head, looking her up and down.

"Better than all those goose-pimpled girls at Brighton," said the Left Head, who had not felt really happy at the seaside.

"When's the wedding?" asked the Right Head.

But this, of course, started all the unhappiness off again, and the lovers went back to the business of sighing and looking into each other's eyes, leaving the ogre and Mr. Leadbetter to explain the events that had led up to this day.

The Wizard Watcher did what it could to cheer everybody up, but after half an hour during which the

Kraken kept trying to climb up its tail, Sir Simon told it in horrid detail what Lady Olivia had said to the lavatory attendant, and Arriman had declared for the hundredth time that he would die without Belladonna, the monster had had enough.

"Proper carry-on in here," said the Middle Head. "It's worse than Blackpool."

"Let's go out and get some fresh air," said the Right Head.

"Good idea," said the Left Head. "Get that little perisher off our tail, anyway."

And twitching the Kraken carefully onto the floor, the monster waddled out into the park.

An hour passed. Mr. Leadbetter had made a list of police stations and was just about to pick up the phone to try again for news of Terence, when they heard the great oak door in the hall burst open with a resounding crash. Next came the sound of footsteps pounding upstairs; then the drawing room door flew open as if pushed by a hurricane and the Wizard Watcher came skidding into the room. Its heads were trembling, its eyes were blazing, and they could actually *see* its heart pounding in its chest. Never had anyone known the monster in such a state, and for a moment its excitement was such that it simply could not speak. Then the Middle Head began and the other two joined in.

"The new wizard cometh!"

"He *cometh!*"

"Right *now*, he cometh!"

Arriman rose with shaking knees and went to the window, and everybody followed him.

Stumbling with exhaustion, his small face lifted to the windows of the hall, Terence Mugg was coming up the drive.

CHAPTER 20

*A*RE YOU SUGGESTING we don't know our job?" said the Middle Head, looking very hurt.

"Yes, are you? I mean, you *made* us, you know," said the Left Head.

"No, no, my dear fellow," said Arriman, who knew how sensitive the monster was. "It's just . . . well, you see, this is Leadbetter's nephew. We've all been rather anxious about him. Of course you haven't met him, you were away during the contest, but that's who it is. Terence's the name. Terence Mugg."

Terence was sitting on the sofa next to Belladonna, who had rushed up to him, half carrying him into the room, and was now feeding him with cauliflower soup and bananas, pale things she'd been able to magic up quickly till Lester could get to the kitchen and rustle up a steak.

Now he stood up. Already being with the people he loved had made his cheeks glow and chased the weariness from his face.

"Actually, sir," he began. "Actually, I think maybe—" But here he broke off because it was so difficult to explain. He didn't really believe it himself yet and had walked all the way from Todcaster rather than try anything that might not work and prove him wrong. So instead he felt in his pocket and took out a piece of string, an apple core, an India rubber—and at last a blue tin punched with holes.

Terence opened the tin. Inside it was a small spider with hairy legs and a black cross on its back.

"What is it?" asked Arriman as they all craned forward.

Terence swallowed.

"It's . . . Matron, sir," he said.

So then he began to explain, growing more confident as his story unfolded. And as he talked it all became quite clear, and the only surprising thing was that no one had suspected it before.

He began by telling what he'd overheard at the home, and as he spoke they could see the tiny baby carried in and snapping at Matron with his full set of teeth so that she had hated him bitterly from that day. They could see a small boy who never cried because wizards, like witches, cannot shed tears, but a small boy who knew nothing of his powers because unlike Mr. and Mrs. Canker, who had wisely encouraged their little Arriman, Terence had grown up in a place where people were ignorant and blind.

And then, when he'd first met Belladonna, Terence went on, he'd felt—oh, not just that he loved her ("Everyone," said Terence, "loves Belladonna.") but a sort of feeling of *belonging,* and from the first moment, when she'd tried to root Matron, Terence had said her spells along with her and worked with her and *felt* with her. "Whatever she did," he said, "I had to do it, and sometimes I said extra spells of my own. Only I thought it was Rover the blackness came from—we both did. I was *sure* it was Rover. But then I met Ms. Leadbetter and she told me that Mr. Moon had never come to the hall at all, he'd had an accident. But Sir Simon *did* appear, and I knew it couldn't be Rover because Rover had already gone. So—"

But this part was news to Lester and Mr. Leadbetter, and gobbledegook to Arriman and Belladonna, and Terence had to stop while everybody explained everything to everyone else. Arriman was most displeased to think that his servants had tried to play a trick on him, but when they explained that it was only because they were so sure that Belladonna was the wife for him, he couldn't really make a fuss.

"Anyway," Terence went on, "I couldn't understand *what* had happened because I knew Belladonna was quite white without the earthworm. So if it wasn't Rover and it wasn't her, who was it? And then when they said that about me biting so hard when I was a tiny baby, everything sort of clicked into place, and when Matron came charging upstairs at me, I just shut my eyes and—well, there she is."

And he held out the tin inside which the spider was scuttling dementedly to and fro.

The rejoicing after Terence had finished his story may be imagined. Belladonna hugged him and kissed him; Lester seized a saber and gulped it down joyfully in a single swallow; Arriman came and pumped him by the hand.

"My dear, dear boy, what happiness, what joy! What a relief! Don't you see, all our problems are solved. You shall stay here and attend to wizardry and darkness, and Belladonna and I can be married and live happily ever after!"

"Oh, Arry, so we can, so we can!" cried Belladonna, rushing into his arms. "It doesn't matter what color our babies are now, does it, with a mighty wizard like Terence to take charge of things?"

"Am I really going to be a *mighty* wizard?" said Terence, his eyes shining.

Arriman turned to him, his dark face serious for a moment.

"You have a great gift, my boy," he said. "A great gift. Necromancy at your age! I couldn't have touched it. Why, if I called the thunder before the lightning I was as pleased as punch. No, it's my belief you're going to extend the frontiers of wizardry and darkness to unheard-of depths. Of course, there's a lot of work before you, but you understand that, I'm sure."

"Oh, yes, sir; I'll work like *anything.*"

In the excitement and happiness which followed, everyone was careful to give the Wizard Watcher his due, and the useful monster sat there, contented smiles on its faces, receiving the congratulations it knew it had deserved.

"Yes, it's a relief," said the Middle Head, nodding graciously. "No use pretending it isn't."

"Those nine hundred and ninety days just sitting

there took it out of us," said the Left Head, "not to mention the chilblains."

"Still, all's well that ends well," said the Right Head.

There was only one slight snag which Mr. Leadbetter, drawing aside his employer, pointed out to Arriman.

"If Sir Simon's real, sir, which it seems he is, what's to become of him? Because it's my belief that if anyone else has to hear about Lady Mary or Lady Julia or Lady Letitia who guzzled, there'll be murder done, and it won't be him doing it."

Arriman nodded. A look of deep wickedness had come into his fiery eyes.

"Actually, Leadbetter, I have just had a very neat idea about Sir Simon. A very neat idea indeed. But first we must have our wedding party. I want you to invite everybody. All the witches that took part in the contest, for a start."

"Even the enchantress, sir?" said Mr. Leadbetter, frowning.

Arriman smiled.

"*Particularly* the enchantress," he said.

CHAPTER 21

THE DAY OF the wedding dawned, and from all over the land there came kobbolds and kelpies, goblins and noggles, furies and fiends, to share the magician's happiness and to meet the new wizard whose coming had been foretold by the gypsy Esmeralda and whose power was said to be greater even than Arriman's own.

No handsomer couple than the bridal pair could be imagined. Arriman was in antlers and a gold-patterned cloak; Belladonna's ink black dress was loose and flowing and in her glorious hair she wore only a single, simple bat. It was the little short-eared bat that had invented an Aunt Screwtooth for her at the coven, and it had flown up specially to be with her on her great day.

In the center of the table, on a blue velvet cushion that the ogre had fitted with a special sprinkler, lay

Rover, looking rosy and peaceful now that it was understood that he was not a powerful familiar but just an ordinary worm. Opposite him in a high chair sat the Kraken, squeaking with excitement. Belladonna had managed to put him into nappies in spite of his eight legs, and with his underneath wrapped in snow-white muslin, he looked, as Terence said, almost like a bridesmaid or perhaps a page.

None of their friends had failed them. Mr. Chatterjee had flown back from Calcutta; the ghoul had left his slaughterhouse. Even Ms. Leadbetter, though she didn't hold with magic, was there, bringing news of the Sunnydene Home's new Matron, a fat and friendly lady whom the children loved. (The old Matron had been let loose in the rose garden, where she was making herself useful eating aphids and other insect pests, as spiders will.)

And the witches were there. However much they had sneered at Belladonna, now that she was Mrs. Canker and Wizardess of the North, they were only too ready to be friendly.

Belladonna, of course, forgave them everything. Not only that, but when the feasting and roistering had died down a little, she laid a hand on Arriman's arm and said: "Arry, shouldn't we grant everyone a wish? Isn't that the thing to do at weddings?"

"Well, my treasure, if that's what you want. Of

course, granting wishes isn't exactly *black*. Still, on such a happy day . . . We'll get Terence to do it; it'll be good practice."

It would take too long to tell what all the brownies and kelpies and noggles wanted, and anyway it was mostly money. Mr. Chatterjee didn't need a wish because he'd tracked down the Princess Shari (the one who'd been a penguin) and was engaged to be married. The ghoul and Ms. Leadbetter didn't hold with wishes, and Ethel Feedbag had fallen asleep with her head on her plate and couldn't be roused.

But Mother Bloodwort knew exactly what *she* wanted.

"It's that turning-myself-young-again spell," she said to Terence. "I can't get it right myself, but you can. About twenty, I'd like to be, or maybe eighteen. Gladys Trotter, the name was, and I'd like to be dressed nice."

But when the wish had been granted and Mother Bloodwort stood staring into the mirror at the young girl she had been, a very odd look spread across her face.

"I don't like it," she said at last. "I'm sorry, but you'll have to turn me back again. All that swollen flesh and those bulgy pink cheeks . . . And what did I want all that hair *for*?"

So Terence turned her back again, and the old woman went back contentedly to her shack, where she lived for many more years being sometimes a coffee table and sometimes a witch, and not doing any harm to anyone because she had forgotten how.

After that it was Mabel Wrack's turn and what *she* wanted was to have her legs turned back into a mermaid's tail. She said she was sick of them itching and sick of humping Doris about in polyethylene buckets and she felt bad, she said, about the way she had treated her aunts. "For when all's said and done, water's thicker than blood and you can't beat a wet family," said Mabel, "so if you'll drop me off at that bit of cliff where I did my trick, I'll find them soon enough."

So the wedding guests, glad of some fresh air after all that eating, trooped off to the Devil's Cauldron, and Terence gave Mabel a splendid tail and two gill slits for breathing underwater, and Belladonna kissed Doris lovingly above her vile red eyes. And sure enough, as Mabel hit the waves, they could all see, distinctly, a set of plump and motherly arms pulling the witch and her octopus down into the foam.

But when Nancy Shouter told the little boy what *she* wanted, Terence turned pale. For what Nancy wanted was no less than the impossible. She wanted Terence to reverse the bottomless hole, to turn it inside out and see if somewhere in its bottomlessness, her sister Nora might be found.

"I don't know if I can do that," said Terence anxiously.

But with Arriman's hand reassuringly on his shoulder, he walked bravely to the east lawn, and the wedding guests followed.

If anyone had doubted up to then that Terence was a great and mighty wizard, they did not doubt again. For Terence just walked up to the hole with its notices saying DANGER and KEEP OUT and took them down. Next, with his shoes, he scuffed out the pentacle of protection. And then he stepped forward and spoke to the hole.

No one heard the words he used. What passed between him and it remains secret till the end of time. But the hole obeyed him; it knew its master—and with a frightful scream, a roaring judder, and a fearful lurch, it gave up its bottomlessness, turned inside out, and from its newfound bottom, dredged up the crumpled, bewildered body of Nancy Shouter's twin.

"Nora!" cried Nancy, rushing forward and sending her chickens flying.

"Nancy!" cried Nora, rushing into her sister's arms.

Taking no notice of anyone, the two sisters stood there, hugging each other and laughing for joy.

Then: "You look a proper mess," said Nancy Shouter. "You're all crumpled."

"Of course I'm crumpled, you stupid stick," said Nora. "What do you expect? You shouldn't have pushed me into the hole in the first place."

"I didn't push you; you fell."

"I didn't."

"You did."

And quarreling happily, the two sisters picked up their chickens and walked away.

But when Terence, carried shoulder-high by the wedding guests, got back to the banqueting hall to grant the enchantress *her* wish, he found her chair empty except for a pair of moth-eaten stays which she had bought in the Portobello Road and poisoned in her parlor. Madame Olympia, it seemed, had returned to London—and with her had gone no less a person than Sir Simon Montpelier!

"So my plan worked!" said Arriman gleefully, rubbing his hands.

"I'll say it worked," said the ogre. "I put the love philter in each of their drinks like you told me, and you should have seen them! The plasher down on his knees asking her to marry him and measuring her neck for a noose at the same time. And her accepting him and trying to get a squint at his molars to see how they'd look on her necklace. I nearly died!"

"A well-matched pair," said Arriman. "I wonder which of them will knock the other off first." He turned to Belladonna. "Am I not clever, my little kitten?"

And Belladonna, gazing at him adoringly, said: "The cleverest person in the world!"

But the best part of any party is the bit where the guests have gone and the family is left alone, tired and content.

Terence lay on the hearth rug, chatting to Rover; Lester was sharpening his bedtime sword. Arriman had

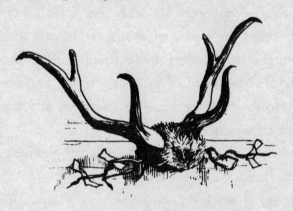

taken off his antlers, and he and Belladonna were curled up on the sofa making plans. They were going to build a little house on the other side of the park—quite close to the hall but not too close, so that Terence would learn to manage on his own. Arriman was going to write a book and Mr. Leadbetter was already wondering how to stop the magician jumbling up the pages and getting the typewriter ribbon jammed and putting the carbon paper in the wrong way around.

So happy and peaceful did everybody feel that it was quite a while before they noticed that the Wizard Watcher wasn't quite itself. Its round and beautiful eyes were suspiciously moist and it was allowing the Kraken to slide down its tail as though it didn't really care what happened.

"Is anything the matter?" asked Arriman. Now he came to think of it, the Watcher hadn't really been itself at the party. It'd eaten hardly anything, and talking had seemed an effort.

The monster shook its head.

"It's nothing," said the Middle Head in a low voice.

"Not anything, really," said the Left Head.

"We're only making a fuss," the Right Head agreed.

By this time, of course, everyone was desperate, and Terence, who had loved the monster from the moment he saw it, put down Rover and came over, quite pop-eyed with concern.

"Please!" said Arriman. "You must tell us! That's what friends are for. To share things with."

The monster sighed heavily.

"Well," said the Middle Head. "It's obvious really, isn't it?"

"I mean, what are Wizard Watchers *for*?" said the Left Head.

"They're for watching for wizards, aren't they?" put in the Right Head.

"So when a wizard's been *found*," said the Middle Head, "there isn't much use for a Wizard Watcher, is there?"

"Sort of *spare*, a Wizard Watcher is then, isn't he?" said the Left Head.

"You could say useless. Redundant. Finished," said the Right Head, dashing away a tear.

There was an absolutely ghastly silence while everyone took in the monster's grief and pain.

Then Belladonna stepped forward, her eyes alight.

"How *could* you be so foolish?" she said to the three heads. "Surely you know that Wizard Watchers aren't just for watching FOR wizards? They're for watching OVER wizards. I thought everyone knew that!"

The monster lifted its heads.

"Terence may be a mighty and terrible wizard, but he's a very young one," Belladonna went on, while the little boy nodded eagerly.

"And skinny with it," said the Middle Head.

"Undernourished, you could say," said the Right Head.

"Short of sleep, I shouldn't wonder," said the Left Head.

"It's my belief a cup of warm milk in the middle of the day wouldn't hurt," said the Middle Head.

"Nor some hot soup at night. You can't beat hot soup, I always say."

"And plenty of fresh air . . ."

Everyone sighed with relief. The monster had withdrawn into a corner, busy and interested, and they could hear it working out a routine in which a young wizard could blight and smite and blast and wither, but *sensibly*.

"You'll be all right now," said Belladonna, drawing the little boy close.

And the wizard who in years to come would be known as Mugg the Magnificent, Flayer of the Foolish and Master of the Shades, looked up at her with shining mud-colored eyes and said:

"Oh, yes! There'll be no one in the world as all right as me!"

TURN THE PAGE FOR A SPECIAL
PREVIEW OF THE NEWEST FANTASY
FROM EVA IBBOTSON,

ISLAND OF THE AUNTS

When the kindly old aunts decide that they need help caring for the mermaids, selkies, and other creatures who live on their hidden island, they know that adults can't be trusted. What they need are a few special children who can keep a secret—a secret as big as a magical island. And what better way to get children who can keep really big secrets, than to kidnap them! (After all, some children just plain need to be kidnapped.) But when the children arrive, not even the aunts can believe the amazing and wondrous things that start to happen!

CHAPTER 1

MINETTE WOKE UP in a strange bed with a lumpy mattress and brass knobs. She was in a big room; shabby, with a threadbare carpet and faded wallpaper in a pattern of parrots and swirling leaves. The curtains breathed slightly in the open windows. A high, mewing noise came from outside.

Then she remembered what had happened, and at once she was very frightened indeed.

She had been eating a sandwich, sitting opposite a strange, fierce aunt who was supposed to be taking her to her father; and suddenly the compartment started going round and round, and the face of the aunt came closer and then farther away . . . and then nothing more. Blackness.

She had been drugged and kidnapped, she was sure of that. She could remember the way the dreadful aunt had peered at her as if she was looking into her soul. Minette knew all about fear, but now she was more afraid than she had ever been. What dreadful fate lay in wait for her? Would they cut off her ear and send it to her parents—or starve her until she did what they wanted?

And what *did* they want? Kidnapping was about getting money out of people, and neither her mother nor her father was rich.

Moving in the bed, she found she was not tied up, but the windows would be barred and the door locked.

Pushing aside the bedclothes, she walked over to the window. She was wearing her own nightdress; the aunt must have kidnapped her suitcase as well. The window was open, and as Minette looked out she gasped with surprise.

For she was looking at a most incredible view. Down below her was green, sheep-cropped turf studded with daisies and eyebright. A large goose with black legs walked across it, followed by six goslings with their necks stretched out. Beyond the turf the ground sloped to a bay of perfect white sand—and then came the sea.

Minette looked and looked and looked. The sea in the morning light was like a crystal mirror; she could hear the waves turning over quietly on the beach. There were three black rocks guarding the bay, and on them she could make out the dark round heads of seals. White birds circled and mewed, and the air smelled of seaweed and shellfish and wind. It smelled of the sea!

"Oh, it's beautiful," she whispered.

But of course she would not be allowed to go outside. Kidnapped children were kept in dark cupboards and blindfolded. Any minute now someone would come and deal with her. She looked round the room. Old furniture, patchwork rugs, and by the bed—and this was odd—a night-light. She had begged and begged for one at home, but neither her father nor her mother had ever let her have one.

A small snuffling sound made her turn quickly. It had come from behind a screen, covered in cutouts of animals, in the corner of the room.

A fierce dog to guard her? But the noise had not been at all a fierce one.

Her heart pounding, she tiptoed to the screen and looked round it. On a camp bed lay a boy of about her own age. He had very dark hair and sticking-out ears, and he was just waking up.

"Who are you?" he asked, staring at her with big round eyes.

"I'm Minette. And I think I've been kidnapped by an aunt."

The boy sat up. "Me too." He blinked. "Yes, I'm sure. I was supposed to be going back to my grandparents. She gave me a hamburger."

"Mine gave me a cheese-and-tomato sandwich."

The boy got out of bed and stretched. He, too, was

wearing his own pajamas. "We'll have to try and escape," he said. "We'll have to."

"Yes. Only I think we're on an island. Come and look."

She didn't know why, but she had had the feeling at once that the sea wasn't just in front of them but all around.

"Wow!" Fabio, too, was struck by the view. "What a place."

Minette had gone over to the door. "Look, it isn't locked!"

"I'm going out," said the boy. "They don't seem to have taken our clothes away. They're crummy kidnappers."

"Unless it's all a trap." She thought of the films she had seen—holes suddenly opening in the floor with pools of man-eating piranhas or sharks below. "Do you think they've kidnapped us to feed us to something?"

He shrugged. "You'd think they'd choose fatter children than us. Come on, get dressed. I'm going out."

There was no one in the corridor; there was no one on the stairs.

Then, from behind a door across the hallway, they heard a scream, followed by a thump, and then a second scream. Someone in there was being tortured—and it sounded like a child.

Minette leaned back against the wall, white-faced and trembling.

"Come on—quick!" Fabio clutched her arm.

The children ran out across the turf, over the dunes, along the perfect crescent of sand. The tide was out; it was a shell beach; there were Venus shells and cowries and green stones polished like emeralds. No one stopped them; there was no one to be seen. It would have been like Paradise except for that ghastly scream.

"Look," said Fabio.

A group of seals had swum toward the shore and was looking at them, swimming in a semicircle, snorting and blowing. . . . With their round heads they looked like a group of Russian dolls.

The children were silent, looking at the seals, and the seals stared back at them. Then suddenly they turned and swam back into the deep water.

All except one, a bull seal with white markings on the throat, who came close to the shore, and closer, until he was in the shallows with his flippers resting in the sand.

"It's as if he's trying to tell us something."

"He's got incredible eyes," said Minette dreamily. "He doesn't look like a seal at all. He looks as though inside he's a person."

"Well, seals are persons. Everything that's alive is a person really."

But that wasn't what she'd meant.

They took off their shoes and walked on the firm wet sand between the tidemarks toward a cliff covered with nesting kittiwakes and puffins and terns. The tide was still going out, leaving behind its treasures: pieces of driftwood as smooth as velvet, crimson crab shells, bleached cuttlefish bones, whiter than snow. There was no sign of any ship. They might have been alone in the universe.

"What's that noise?" asked Fabio, stopping suddenly.

A deep and mournful sound, a kind of honking, had come from somewhere inland.

"It must be a foghorn," said Minette.

But there wasn't any fog, or any lighthouse to give warning if there had been.

They listened for a few moments but the sound did not come again, and they ran on along the shore. It was a marvelous island; it seemed to have everything. To their left was a green hill; two hills, actually, with a dip between, the slopes covered with bracken and gorse. The far shore would be wilder, exposed to the wind.

"If we climbed up there, we could see exactly where we are. There might be other islands or a causeway. If we're going to escape, we're going to have to know," said Minette.

They had to get away—that terrible scream still rang in their ears—but Minette couldn't help thinking of where she would be if she hadn't been kidnapped, in her father's dark sitting room trying to get interested in a book until he came back from the university.

Fabio seemed to be having the same sort of thoughts. "I can't help wondering if my grandparents will pay the ransom for me. They're horribly cheap and they don't like me."

Minette tried to think if her parents liked her enough to pay a lot of money to get her back, but when she thought about her parents, her stomach always started to lurch about, so she said, "There's a little path there to the top of the hill."

They began to run toward the gap in the dunes, forgetting the lives they had left behind, forgetting even that awful tortured scream. The wind was at their backs; it was like flying. No one could imagine anything dangerous or dark.

And then it happened! From behind the hummock of sand that had hidden them, there arose suddenly the cruel figures of two enormous women.

It was the evil aunts!

The sinister kidnappers glared at the children, and the children, terrified, stared back. Here was the tall bony aunt with her fierce eyes who had drugged Minette's sandwich, and here was the plump mad person with her scarves flying in the wind who had given sleeping powders to a defenseless boy.

The children reached for each other's hands. Minette was shaking so much she could hardly stand. What punishment would they be given for escaping from their room?

It was the tall bony aunt, Etta, who spoke. "You're late for breakfast," she said in her fierce and booming voice.

The children continued to stare.

"Breakfast," the other one went on. "You've heard of that? We have it at seven, and the cook gets ratty if he's kept waiting. Go and wash your hands first—the bathroom's at the top of the stairs."

The children ran off, completely puzzled by this way of kidnapping people, and Etta and Coral followed. They were talking about Myrtle, who hadn't stopped crying since she came back.

"She's got to stop blaming herself," said Coral. "Mistakes can happen to anyone."

"Yes. Mind you, Lambert is quite a mistake!"

Breakfast was in the dining room, a big room with shabby leather chairs, which faced the patch of green turf and the bay. All the windows in the L-shaped farmhouse had at least a glimpse of the sea. Even the bathroom, with its huge claw-footed bath and ancient geyser, looked out on the ledge of rock where the seals hauled out of the water to rest.

"Porridge or cereal?" asked Aunt Etta as the children came in.

Minette blinked at her. "Cereal," she managed to say.

"Porridge," said Fabio.

"Please," said Etta briskly, picking up the ladle. "Porridge, *please*."

242

Fabio was the first to shake himself awake. "This is a very odd kidnap," he said crossly. "And I won't eat anything drugged."

Aunt Etta leaned forward, scooped a spoonful of porridge from his plate, and gulped it down.

"Satisfied?" she said.

Fabio waited to see if she yawned or became dopey. Then he began to eat. The porridge was delicious.

They were both on second helpings when the screams began again. This time they were even worse than before and were followed by sobs and wails and a low shuddering moan. Then the door opened and a woman they had never seen before ran into the room. She had long, reddish gray hair down her back; a bloody scratch ran along one cheek, and she seemed to be quite beside herself.

The children shrank back in their chairs, their fear returning. The woman looked every inch a torturer.

"Really, Myrtle," said Aunt Etta, "I've told the children they mustn't be late for breakfast, and now look at you."

But no one could be cross with Myrtle for long, not even her bossy sister. The scratch on Myrtle's cheek had begun to bleed again, there were tooth marks on her wrist, and though she took a helping of porridge, she was quite unable to swallow it.

And when she was introduced to Minette and Fabio, her tears began to flow again.

"Yours are so nice," she sobbed. "They look so intelligent and friendly."

"That's as may be," said Etta. "We haven't tried them out yet." She frowned as more bangs and thumps came from across the corridor. "He can't stay in the broom cupboard, Myrtle. What would happen if he goes for the vacuum cleaner? We'd never get the place cleaned up again."

"It's just for now," said Myrtle. "I gave him my bedroom when he first came round, but I was afraid for the ducklings."

Myrtle often had motherless ducklings keeping warm in her bed and her underclothes drawer.

"I suppose we shall have to *un*kidnap him," said Coral. "But how? No one's going to pay a ransom for Lambert Sprott."

"We could offer to *give* his father some money if he'll take Lambert away," suggested Myrtle, blowing her nose.

"Don't be silly, Myrtle," said Etta. "For one thing, we haven't got any money—and for another, he'd tell everyone about the Island and photographers would come, and journalists." She shuddered. Keeping the position of the Island secret was the most important thing of all.

"We could turn him round and round until he was completely giddy and leave him in a telephone kiosk somewhere on the mainland," said Coral. But she did not sound very convinced by her idea.

Myrtle began to sob again. "I should have left him on the floor," she gulped. "I should never have brought him. But it seemed so cruel just to leave him there unconscious."

"Hush. What's done is done."

But Myrtle couldn't be consoled. "And my cello case smells of the awful child," she wailed. "He puts terrible, perfumed stuff on his hair."

"Perhaps he'll settle down when we've got some breakfast into him."

Judging by the screams and thumps coming from across the corridor, though, this did not seem likely.

But Fabio was getting impatient. "What about *us*? Are you going to unkidnap us?"

The aunts stared at him. "Are you mad?" said Etta. "After all the trouble we took. In any case, you haven't been kidnapped exactly. You've been *chosen*."

Minette and Fabio stared. "How?" asked Minette.

"What do you mean?" enquired Fabio.

Aunt Coral put down her coffee cup. "It's time we explained. But first you'd better come and meet Daddy. He gets upset when things are kept from him."

Captain Harper was a hundred and three years old and spent most of the day in bed looking at the Island through his telescope.

He was very deaf and very grumpy, and what he

saw through the window didn't please him. When he was young, there had been far more geese coming from Greenland—hundreds and thousands of geese—and their feet had been yellower and their bottoms more feathery than the geese that came nowadays. The sheep had been fleecier when he was a boy, and the flowers in the grass had been brighter, and the seals on the rocks ten times larger and fatter.

"Huge, they were," Captain Harper would say, throwing out his arms. "Great big cow seals with big bosoms and eyes like cartwheels, and look at them now!"

No one liked to say that it was partly because he couldn't see or hear too well that things had changed, and when he told the same stories for the hundredth time, his daughters just smiled and tiptoed out of the room, because they were fond of him and knew that being old is difficult.

"Here are the children, Father," yelled Coral. "The ones who have come to stay with us."

The old man put down his telescope and stared at them.

"They're too small," he said. "They won't be a mite of use. You need ones with muscles. When I was their age I had muscles like footballs."

He put out a skinny arm and flexed his biceps, and they could see a bump like a very small pea come up on his arm. "We were all strong in those days. There was a boy in my class who could lift the teacher's desk with one hand. Freddie Boyle he was called. He was the one who put the grass snake down the teacher's trouser leg."

The aunts let him tell the story about the grass snake and the teacher's trouser leg because it was a short one, but when he began on the one about Freddie Boyle's uncle, who'd run over his own false teeth with a milk truck, they shepherded the children out quietly.

"He won't notice," they said.

When they went downstairs again they found Art, the cook, wiping porridge off his trouser leg. He had tried to give Lambert some breakfast and had it thrown in his face.

"Nasty little perisher you've got in there," he said. "Best drown him, I'd say. Shouldn't think his parents would want him back."

Before he escaped and was washed up on the Island, Art had worked in the prison kitchens, which was why he made such good porridge. Because he'd killed a man once, Art didn't like the sight of blood, and it was always the aunts who had to chop the heads off the fish before they went into the frying pan or get the chickens ready for the pot. Another thing Art didn't like to do was anything energetic.

"I don't know my own strength," he would say when there was anything messy or difficult to be done. "I might forget myself and do someone an injury."

This didn't seem likely—Art was a skinny person who hardly came up to Aunt Etta's shoulder—but he'd quickly locked the door on Lambert and, leaving him to scream for his mobile telephone, retreated to his kitchen.

But Aunt Etta and Aunt Coral now led the children into the garden behind the house. It was time to explain.

The garden was surrounded by gray walls to give shelter from the wind; but no walls on the Island were built so high that they shut out the view of the sea. Aunt Myrtle had gone down to play her cello to the seals. A bumblebee droned on a clump of thrift. It was very peaceful.

"Perhaps I'd better tell you a story," said Etta. "It's a true story and it begins with five girls coming to an island with their widowed father to look for a new life.

"They found a lovely and deserted place, but ruined, abandoned. All the people who had lived there had left long, long ago. Even the ghost in the old graveyard seemed to have gone away."

Minette sat with her arms hugging her knees and her eyes closed. She loved stories.

"So the girls and their father repaired the house and planted a garden and learned to fish and cut peat and do all the things the Islanders had done before they left. But of course the world outside was changing. Oil was spilled into the sea, and sewage, and trawlers started to use nets that caught even the smallest fish. The water became overheated by nuclear power stations. You'll have learned all that at school."

Minette nodded, but Fabio only scowled. Absolutely nothing useful had been taught at Greymarsh Towers.

"Soon the sisters and their father found themselves looking after things that came ashore. Oiled seabirds . . . stunned seals . . . poisoned squids . . . and other things . . ."

Etta paused and looked up at Coral, who raised her eyebrows in a warning way. *Not yet,* said Coral's eyebrows. *Remember what we decided.*

Etta nodded and turned back to the children.

"The sisters worked from dawn to dusk. One of them was an idiot; she started shaving her legs and marrying tax inspectors, so she was no good. And one went off to foreign parts to stop people eating rare animals. And the others got older and became aunts. . . .

"And then one day they realized they might die before long—they might become extinct—and then what would happen to all the creatures? So they decided to find people to carry on after them. Sensible people. Young ones. People who knew how to work."

There was a long pause. Then:

"Us?" said Fabio shyly.

Both aunts nodded.

"Yes," said Aunt Etta. "You."

Eva Ibbotson has published many popular, award-winning novels in Great Britain. Her first book published in the United States, *The Secret of Platform 13* (Dutton and Puffin), was named a *School Library Journal* Best Book of the Year and one of the New York Public Library's 100 Titles for Reading and Sharing.

Ms. Ibbotson has a daughter and three sons, now grown, who showed her that children like to read about ghosts, wizards, and witches "because they are just like people but madder and more interesting." She lives in England.

Annabel Large has illustrated several books for children. She lives in England.